This book
purchased
with donations
made to the
GiveBIG
for Books
Campaign.

The
Seattle
Public
Library
Foundation

www.foundation.spl.org

# FIGHTING FOR DONTAE

# FIGHTING FOR DONTAE

## Mike Castan

Holiday House / New York

HOLIDAY HOUSE is registered in the U.S. Patent and Trademark Office.
Printed and Bound in February 2012 at Maple Vail, York, PA, USA.
www.holidayhouse.com
First Edition
1  3  5  7  9  10  8  6  4  2

Library of Congress Cataloging-in-Publication Data

Castan, Mike.
Fighting for Dontae / by Mike Castan. — 1st ed.
p. cm.
Summary: When Mexican American seventh-grader Javier is assigned to work
with a special education class and connects with Dontae, who has both physical and
mental disabilities, his reputation among gang members and drug abusers no longer
seems very important.
ISBN 978-0-8234-2348-4 (hardcover)
[1. Conduct of life—Fiction.  2. People with disabilities—Fiction.
3. People with mental disabilities—Fiction.  4. Mexican Americans—
Fiction.  5. Middle schools—Fiction.  6. Schools—Fiction.  7. Family
problems—Fiction.  8. California—Fiction.]  I. Title.
PZ7.C268586Fig 2012
[Fic]—dc23
2011042115

*From one at-risk student
to another*

*—M. C.*

# FIGHTING
# FOR DONTAE

# CHAPTER I

Route 66 is a famous old highway that used to run all the way across the country. Back in fourth-grade social studies, I learned that the route started out in Chicago and ran clear to Los Angeles. Along the way there were tons of towns where people would stop for gas, food, and lodging. Then little by little, new highways sprang up and the route was forgotten. It got broken up, bulldozed over, and in some places left for dead.

My town is on the western end of what's left of that famous old highway. It's in California, but it isn't the California that you see on TV or in the movies. Far away from the neighborhoods of East LA is Orbe Nuevo. From what the old people say, Orbe Nuevo at one time had been nothing but orange groves and grape vineyards from end to end. Nowadays it isn't anything like that. It's just miles and miles of tract houses, and then a strip mall or two, and then miles and miles of tract houses again. Every now and then you'll come across a few rows of run-down apartments. Usually, there'll be some little kids playing on top of some broken-down cars out front. When I was little, one of those kids might have been me.

Since then, though, I'd seen most of my friends drift away.

By the time I made it to middle school, I already felt like a survivor. The only friends I knew that were still around were Eduardo, Jesse, and Desi. Everybody else was gone. Pretty soon, I started thinking that friends weren't meant to stay, that they were just people to know for a short time. For a couple of friends, the California State Youth Authority, or YA, was where they went. For a few others a vampire called crystal meth came along and sucked all the life out of them. Funny how something that looks as harmless as baking soda could make a person disappear on you, but that's what happened. And still other friends just moved away.

For some reason Eduardo, Jesse, Desi, and I stuck around. It was almost impossible to be a guy in my town and not belong to a gang, so we joined one. It all happened one night a couple of years back in a vacant lot near an old factory. Six Southside Playaz whupped us up like we'd never been whupped before. After it was over, they started calling us homeboys. Just like that, we were in. But it didn't change all that many things for us. The next day we still had to go to school. We still got sent to the principal's office when we got too wild. We still had to go home and get whupped by our parents. So nothing really changed. But we were in a gang.

Being in a gang meant you had to stand up for your set. We hadn't been asked to do anything hard-core for the Playaz yet, but we did have to defend our turf—a little block south of the chaparral between First and J Avenues. That included the apartment complex my mom and I lived in and the little tract houses where my friends lived. We couldn't let the North-siders mess around in our turf, like tag it or trespass or talk to any of the girls. Well, maybe we weren't very good gangsters or something, but none of the guys or I spent too much time doing that. I think we mostly just joined the gang because we thought that was what we were supposed to do. At school we got some respect for being in the Playaz, but otherwise there weren't too many perks.

Of course, I wore my gang uniform most days, which was a white T-shirt and baggy jeans, until the school district banned gang attire on school grounds. Then it became a game of how to dress like one of the Playaz but still not break the dress code. Most of us would just wear a sweatshirt or jacket over our white tees throughout the day and pull up our pants really high. And then once school was out, we'd take off our sweatshirts and let our baggies drop. I kept my head shaved so I'd look like the rest of the guys. But if it weren't for that, you wouldn't think for a second that I belonged to a gang.

Soon after we were jumped in, the school district police started paying real close attention to us. If Eduardo, Jesse, Desi, and I were walking home together, they'd drive real slow behind us. A couple of times the police even stopped us to check our pockets for tagging markers and stuff. When they'd do that, they'd always ask us a list of questions, like "Are any of you in a gang?" and "Where were you last night?" The guys and I knew the routine, so we would always play it cool.

A part of me felt like it was really dumb to be dressing the way we were, and acting the way we did, and being Playaz and all. It was like we were wearing a red flag and telling everybody that we were trouble, like in a way we were asking to be stopped by the cops and stuff, but I never said anything about the way I felt. That was something you just couldn't do, ever.

If you were a guy and Latino in my town, you'd come off as a punk or soft if you talked about your feelings.

But I thought about it so much that I'd imagined running away to leave it all behind—not the gang, but everything. I mean, there were some things that were too embarrassing for anybody to know—like the fact that my pop was in jail.

If I had to describe my pop, I guess I'd say that he was restless: He was always on his way to, or coming from, jail. I'd only see him for small periods of time, like a few weeks, and then he'd be gone. Sometimes he'd be in county lockup for a few months, and other times he'd be in the state pen for a few years. It was like my dad couldn't really exist outside of jail.

For those short periods of time when he was home, from what I remembered, it was always fun and cool . . . for the first week or so. Then little by little, he'd change. His first couple of days home, he would be up early making breakfast, with a clean shirt on, a shave, and a sparkle in his eyes. He'd be excited and talking about how he had a line on a job, and that if he got it, things would be good. But he never would get that job. Then a few days later, the clean shirt would become a T-shirt. A little while after that, he'd stop shaving. And then eventually he wouldn't be awake when I got up for school. My mom would get this real serious look in her eyes, but she'd always cover for him too, saying stuff like he wasn't feeling well. Then pop would start to come home late at night, usually high. He and my mom would fight, sometimes for hours, with doors slamming and dishes breaking. I'd stay in my room in the dark and listen to them because it wasn't like I could sleep with all that going on. Eventually my pop would stop coming home altogether. Then a couple of weeks after that, the phone would ring from the county jail, and that's when my mom and I would find out what happened to him this time.

My pop would always be sad and sorry over the phone. He'd always tell my mom not to worry about bailing him out, that he didn't want her to waste the money. Then the news would come after a few more weeks that my pop was doing a stint, and that's all I'd see of him until his next release date.

Over the years my pop had done a lot of stints. Sometimes they were for drugs or booze, and other times they were for fighting or stealing. One time he even picked up nine months for assaulting a cop. It never surprised me to hear what my pop had done. And there seemed to be more stories than I could count. My pop had a hard-core reputation. He had grown up in our town, and everybody knew him. Sometimes when he was home between stints and we'd be somewhere, random people would come up to him to shake his hand and say hi. "Hey, man! How you been?" "How long you been out?" "That's cool, man. Take it easy." Other people would look at him with fear, like they knew what he was capable of doing and didn't want any part of it. My pop also had tattoos all up and down his arms and all over his chest, and that was enough to scare some people without anything else. But to me he was just my pop.

Sure, my pop wasn't the only one locked up. But it was embarrassing. To me, getting locked up seemed like the poor, stupid people thing to do. And I didn't want to come off as that, even if that's what I was, so I never really told anybody about him. If anybody ever asked, like a teacher or people at the school office, I'd just tell them he was a truck driver and that he and my mom were separated. Most of the time nobody asked any more questions.

My mom was a checker at a discount store. Most of the kids at school and their families knew her without knowing she was my mom. That wasn't the embarrassing thing about her—she was a tweaker too. I'd probably known since about the third grade. Back then I'd noticed how my mom's moods would change. One minute she'd be down and tired and the next she'd be up and wired. She could be happy and fun and then, a little while later, angry and mean. I never really knew what to expect. Then I started to notice her smoking gear lying around here and there, like her pipe and those little empty plastic baggies.

I wondered for months what they were for. Then one day I asked my mom about them, and she got all defensive and angry. I knew off the bat that it was something bad and that she was ashamed of it. So I left it alone. Over the years I'd seen meth on cop shows and stuff, and some people I knew even picked up smoking it. I saw my friend Juan wither away in less than six months when he started getting high with his older brother. Juan started doing crazy stuff like setting things on fire. And then just a few months ago, he got busted big time and ended up in YA.

I knew meth could wreck you, and I worried about my mom. Lately though, she'd been going to a prayer group to help her get off the stuff. She was doing really good. Things were straightening up. She didn't crash out for long times, and she seemed more there.

You'd think that would be enough for me to want to get away, having parents that were messed up and all, but what really sucked was that we were poor too. We weren't the only poor people I knew. Some kids at school had it worse off than me, and at least we had a TV and food and stuff, because I knew for a fact that some of the kids didn't. Most of us got free meals at schools, but there were some kids that really, really needed them. My mom and I weren't *that* poor, but we were poor enough. We were the kind of poor that made me need to do something drastic a week before school started.

First off, shoes are a big deal in middle school. People know you by your shoes. If you don't have the right ones, your reputation could be sunk just like that. This made sense to me, but there would have been no way to explain it to my mom, especially when we couldn't afford Chuck T's. So I had to take matters into my own hands.

With just one week till school started, I knew I couldn't waste time. The only place I'd have almost a halfway chance of getting away with it would be the Farmers Market, an outdoor swap that was held every Sunday. Why it was called the Farmers Market, I'm not sure. There were never any real farmers there, or animals or anything. But at this market they sold all kinds of things. You could get a new plasma TV, jewelry, clothes—anything. And of course, you could find shoes there too.

So by that Sunday I'd decided to swipe a pair of Chuck T's. I had it all planned out. I even got Eduardo and Desi to be my helpers. We had staked out the Farmers Market a few weeks before. We knew which stand had the shoes I wanted and what stack my size was in. We'd even found a tossed-out bag from the shoe dealer's stand in a trash can in our neighborhood. That would help when we were trying to leave without getting caught. The shoes I'd decided on were a pair of black low tops like all my friends wore. They would've cost thirty-seven dollars plus tax if I was gonna pay for them. And there was no way I could. And I had to have those shoes. So the heist was on.

Jesse would've been cool to go with us, but he did church with his parents every Sunday and couldn't make it. So it was just me, Eduardo, and Desi. I wasn't worried about the guys ratting on me and stuff, because I knew they were cool about things like this. If it had been for anything else, like some girl or some stupid band or TV show, they'd have goofed and clowned at me. But when it came to stuff that really mattered, they'd never rat on me, and they were probably the only other people in the world that understood how done I'd be if I didn't have those shoes. So they were down one hundred percent.

The Sunday morning we were going to the market, I checked in on my mom. She was asleep in her room, out cold. She didn't even stir when I opened the door. I noticed a lighter on the dresser. I figured she'd been partying after work, but it could have just been for cigs, so I didn't think too much about it. I slipped out of our apartment, hit the streets, and met the guys on the corner. Then we were off.

The Farmers Market was a couple of miles south of our neighborhood, on a huge lot next to the freeway. The guys and I had a long walk ahead of us, but they didn't mind. They were busy tagging everything in sight. I let them have fun while I worked over the plan in my head.

When we got to the market, the place was packed. I thought that would be better for us. The more people there were, the easier it would be to swipe the shoes and get out without too much notice.

The guys and I walked through the market and tried to look inconspicuous. We stopped at a few stands to look at stuff before moving on, until we were close to the shoe stand. An

Asian couple ran the stand, and they were really hands-on, asking every customer if they needed help. It was going to be tough, I thought, but we could do it. We just had to wait until there were four or five people there. And when the owners were tied up helping the other people, we'd do our thing.

Patiently we waited by a poster stand and pretended to browse. First there were two people shopping at the shoe stand, and then three. Then another couple walked up. And then a lady with three kids. That was it. It was our time. I nodded to Eduardo, and he nodded to Desi.

According to the plan, Eduardo would divert the Asian couple by making a big deal about finding a certain pair of shoes. While they were distracted I'd grab the box I wanted. Desi was the lookout. He was going to shout, "Let's haul ass!" if anybody caught on.

Like clockwork, Eduardo made his way over to the shoe stand, with Desi and me trailing behind. Then Eduardo started to act real obsessed, pawing through the shoes on display. Even with all the customers, the Asian lady came over to help him. Eduardo worked it good. When the lady showed him white sneakers, he asked for black. If she showed him high tops, he wanted low tops. If the laces were white, he asked if they had red. As he went on and on with the lady I glanced over at the Asian guy and saw he was helping other people. He didn't even glance at me. Slyly I glided over to the shoulder-high wall of stacked shoe boxes that contained my size. From under my T-shirt, I pulled out the bag the guys and I had found in the trash can and unrolled it.

Hunching down, I finally found the box I wanted right in the middle of the wall of shoe boxes. If I pulled out the box the wrong way, the whole wall would come tumbling down.

"Shit," I mumbled under my breath.

It was too risky. Our whole plan was going down the drain. Peeking up over the wall, I saw Eduardo was still busy with the Asian lady. He caught me looking and shot me a look that said, *Grab it and let's go. I'm running out of stuff to ask her.* My eyes darted over to Desi, who was standing by an ice cream stand across from the shoe stand. His look was similar to Eduardo's, but there was a little more fear in his eyes. Nervously he motioned for me to look at a strolling security guard a few stands away. It was over. We'd get caught for sure. Security guards had two-way radios. Even if this one didn't catch us, he'd radio to the one at the gates that we were coming. And if *he* didn't catch us, he'd have the police there in seconds. Just about to give up, I thought about having to go to school next Monday without Chuck T's. I'd be done before first period of my first day of middle school, and it would be torture nonstop from then on. No matter what, I'd be the kid with the bargain shoes that my mom had gotten with her 15 percent employee discount.

With that fresh on my mind and my heart pounding with fear, I snatched the box and slid it quickly out. Amazingly, the wall held together. I tried to stuff the box into the bag, but I was so nervous, my hand was shaking so much that the lid slipped off the box, and then the shoes popped out and fell to the ground. Panicking, I grabbed them and stuffed them into the bag, crushing the shoes and the box and the lid all together. I stood up straight and saw that Eduardo was just about to get thrown out of the shoe stand. The Asian lady was pointing her finger in his face.

"If you no buy shoes, just go! Leave!"

I glanced over at Desi, and I could tell he was just about to yell out our trouble-alarm because the security guard was starting to look interested in what was going on. I shook my head at Desi, then I tried to slip away unnoticed. Holding the bag casually, like I had bought and paid for the shoes all fair and square, I made it over to him. We waited coolly for Eduardo, who kept arguing with the lady. *Eduardo could be a great actor someday*, I thought as he started blaming her for everything.

"Why don't you want to help me? How come? You just don't like Mexicans! That's why!"

Desi and I were trying hard not to laugh as Eduardo kept going. Soon the security guard was standing between them.

"She don't like Mexicans! That's why she don't want to help me!" he pleaded to the guard, who eyed Eduardo skeptically.

"He no leave! He no buy! He not know what he want!" the Asian lady explained.

"Fine! I'll find my shoes somewhere else!" Eduardo said, then turned around and walked off.

He nodded for us to follow him, and we did. We were steps away when suddenly the whole wall of shoe boxes came tumbling down to the ground. I was too scared to turn back and look, so I just nudged the guys in front of me to keep walking. And that walk out of the Farmers Market seemed like the longest walk of my life. Tons of people were in our way. Every corner seemed to have a security guard standing in it, and they all eyed us as we walked by. I wondered if the call had come through to be on the lookout for us. Maybe they were going to let us get to the gates before they sprung a trap and arrested us for shoplifting. A few of my friends had been popped for shoplifting in the past, and from what I'd heard, it was a big hassle. They had to go to the police station and everything. Then when they got home, they got whupped by their parents. That would be me, I thought as we made it to the gates and saw two security guards standing nearby. Right outside were two city police cars blocking the way to the parking lot. They were there for us. This was it. We were popped.

The guys and I didn't break our stride as we approached the gates. The two security guards standing there gave us all long looks, but they didn't move. I held the drawstring of the shoe bag tight and swung the bag casually to make it look like I had nothing to hide. As we walked past the guards they didn't say anything. My heart was beating so hard, I was sure that they must have heard it. Then one, two, and three, we made it past the first hurdle. As I was about to walk around the city cops Eduardo, who was in the lead, went right through the middle of the two cars. *Macho Eduardo*, I thought. We're all going to get popped because he wants to look brave. Hesitantly I followed, just waiting to feel a strong hand on my shoulder. But then we were past the cars and in the parking lot. It was a miracle we'd made it!

The whole walk back home was like a party. The guys and I felt so good about our heist that it was nonstop laughter all the way. Eduardo did his best impression of the Asian lady, which kept Desi and me cracking up. I knew that it was wrong to take the shoes, but I had to admit to myself that it felt good to have gotten away with it. If it hadn't been for school coming up, I'd have never done it, I'm sure. And if I had the money, I would've paid for them fair and square. But I didn't, so I hadn't, and now I had the shoes.

When I got home, I went straight to my room to try the Chuck T's on. My mom had left a note saying she went to work and dinner was in the fridge, so I didn't have to worry about her barging in and wondering where the shoes came from. I sat on my bed and loosened the drawstring on the bag. The shoes were still all mixed up with tissue and the pieces of the box. I started getting scared all over again—it could've gone really bad for us if we'd gotten caught. My mom would've been all over me. I hadn't been whupped in a couple of years, but I'm sure she would've started up where she'd left off, with a few weeks restriction thrown in and everything. I sighed when I thought about the mess that could have been.

Carefully I took the shoes out of the bag. They smelled nice. New shoes always smelled too nice to wear, especially since you knew they'd stop smelling like that in a couple of days. I'd have to be careful around my mom. Once they were worn in a little, I could tell her somebody gave them to me because they didn't fit. Sure it was a straight-up lie, but I had to do what would work.

The Chuck T's looked awesome. They were black canvas with little silver vent loops on the inner sides. They had white strings and a white band around the sole. They were old-school all the way, and all the homeboys in the Playaz wore them. It didn't bother me that we would all look the same. If I had something different from the other guys, I'd stand out, and standing out meant I'd be an easy target. Then I'd be a target for everything. I just wanted to blend in so I could see what Orbe Nuevo Middle School was all about. 'Cause to be honest, just the thought of going there was scaring me to death. All I'd heard about it was bad. How was I going to make it when I really got there?

I pushed the thought of Orbe Nuevo Middle out of my mind, and I slipped on the Chuck T's. They fit perfectly. They felt good on my feet. No mirror in our house was low enough for me to get a really good look at them, so I held up a foot to the mirror above the bathroom sink. *Awesome*, I thought as I saw the reflection. At least my feet were ready for middle school even if the rest of me wasn't.

# CHAPTER 2

A whole new place with new faces everywhere and harder classes too. I'd sweated the first day of school all summer long. Of the four middle schools in my town, Orbe Nuevo was the biggest, with lots of buildings and security guards and everything. Five different elementary schools funneled into it, so there'd be kids there that I'd never seen in my life. I only had a handful of friends anyway, so I'd be pretty much all by myself. After orientation a couple weeks back, I'd learned that Eduardo, Desi, and Jesse weren't going to be in hardly any of my classes. I'd only see Eduardo for PE and Desi for science. Jesse was in high achievers, so none of his classes matched mine or the other guys, but I did get to have lunch with him.

Jesse had always been a brain. He'd been in high achievers for as long as I could remember. He'd even do our homework for us if we asked him. He could do his *and* ours faster than we could do ours alone, so sometimes it worked out really well. Other times, like that time in the fifth grade when I got caught turning in something he'd done for me, it could go really bad. We both got into big trouble, and from then on, I always had to dumb down whatever he told me to write, just so it would sound like it came from me.

Jesse had two older brothers who'd always gotten into

trouble, and now they were locked up in prison. Because of them, his parents came down especially hard on him. They were trying to convince him to go into the seminary to become a priest. The guys and I thought this was a big joke 'cause nobody cursed harder or told more dirty jokes than Jesse. He'd smoked cigarettes since he was about ten, and last year he started up on herb. He'd catch a buzz in the bushes on our way home from school sometimes. He said he needed it before having to deal with his parents and his catechism classes. None of the other guys smoked as much herb as Jesse, but we all kind of accepted that he was just the brainy pothead in our set, and that was that.

Me, well, I guess I'd always had trouble with school. From what I'd heard at parent-teacher conferences, I was an underachiever. My state test scores had always been above average, but when it came to doing classwork and homework, I just wouldn't do it. As I sat in class after an assignment was given out, my mind would wander. Usually I'd start thinking about how today seemed like yesterday, and how it was pointless what I did today because my life would never change. I'd still be the Javier whose pop was locked up. I'd still be the Javier whose mom was a tweaker. I'd still be the Javier who lived in the poor section of town. There was no future in being me.

Cs and Ds were my usual grades, and I'd always managed to get them and move on. I never thought I was actually stupid or anything, but I never considered myself smart like Jesse. People like him were born that way. School was meant for people like him.

I knew I'd probably drop out eventually. I didn't think it would be because of drugs, 'cause, well, I didn't really like them. I'd tried to catch a buzz with Jesse a few times, but I didn't like the feeling of not feeling. Even if my feelings were the same every day, at least I knew what they were. When I puffed on some herb, it was like I was nowhere at all.

Then again, I might get caught up in the Playaz and what was going on with them. They were always into some scandalous stuff. Some guys I knew, like Roberto, who was a couple of years older than me, were already doing legwork for them. They had jobs. They'd drop off herb and meth to different houses, then pick up the money for the gang. Even though they weren't old enough to drive, they already had cars and plenty of money. They had steady girlfriends too. Sure, they'd get popped by the cops every now and then and get thrown in juvie or YA, but it seemed like they were free in a way. They didn't worry about tomorrow. A few of the guys even said they'd done hits on people, like killed people and stuff. I didn't know if I actually believed that, but I did know that they didn't stress out over school or their parents. They were living their own lives.

Sometimes I'd run into Roberto on the streets, and he already seemed like a grown-up. His eyes would be cold and have no life in them. He'd never laugh or joke around like we used to just a couple of years back. Whenever I'd see him, I'd always wonder if that would be me. Would I be a dropout, a criminal, a gangster? Rather than fight it, I thought maybe I should just let it happen. I mean, look at my pop.

Course, when it came to school, there were some things I liked. I could journal for hours, even after that part of class had stopped. I liked making up stories about people that never existed. I could make them heroes or villains. I could journal a story about pirates or cowboys or anything. The only part about journaling I didn't like was when the teacher made us write about something boring, but even that was better than regular classwork.

Somehow I'd gotten into reading too. Because I was one of the Playaz and we had to act a certain way all the time, I couldn't really be seen reading, so I would sneak into the library to check out books, or if a teacher was giving away old books, I'd go back after everybody had left for the day and take, like, five. I'd read them most nights before my mom got home from work. We didn't have cable, and asking my mom for a game box would've been like asking her for the moon. So I read.

I could usually mow through a good-sized book in a couple of nights. If the book was too hard for me, like this time I'd found a copy of *A Tale of Two Cities*, I'd read it over a few times until it made sense. That one took me three tries. But then I enjoyed it.

So those were the only two reasons why I showed up at school that first day, reading and journaling. If I'd ditched the first day of middle school, I wouldn't have found out where the library was or if I got to journal in some of my classes or not. So I showed up. And man, was it a zoo. There were thousands of kids. I got lost going to just about all of my classes. I held on to my backpack and class schedule like they were the only two things I owned. And even after looking over my schedule two or three times before going to a class, I would still wind up in the wrong room. There was no help either, because most of the kids were in the same boat as me. Eduardo, Desi, and Jesse were somewhere out there, but I didn't see a sign of them. I figured they must have been struggling too.

That first day of school, all the teachers were hard-core. I didn't dare try to goof off. Here and there I'd spot a kid that I'd gone to elementary with, but they looked just as scared. The eighth-graders were no help at all. They had an attitude like you'd better not even think of talking to them or you'll wind up with a fist in your face. I didn't say anything to anybody. I just played it cool and tried to keep up.

My schedule wasn't too bad. I had English first, then homeroom, and then reading. Fourth period I had social studies, and from there I was supposed to go to work experience, where we learn a work skill by helping out on campus. They hadn't given out assignments yet, so I would have to stay in social studies and do reading again. Lunch was next, and for fifth period I had math, then for sixth I had PE, and then back to my math classroom for science. It seemed impossible to do it all in a day.

Honestly, I thought about ditching as soon as I got to school. I figured I'd go hide out in the wash, just to the east of town. A lot of kids who ditched would hang out there. It was a dry riverbed that ran all the way from the mountains to the sea. I could stay there all day, and then around three thirty I could take off for home. I'd just tell my mom that I'd gone to school. I could probably get away with it for at least a week.

As I approached the gates of Orbe Nuevo Middle, I knew I had to make up my mind. There were so many kids, nobody would notice if I just slipped down the street in the other direction. Then I remembered I wanted to check out the library. So I gave in and walked through the gates slowly, my new Chuck T's on my feet.

First period was English, and I walked in late 'cause I got lost. The teacher had already started, and all the kids turned to look when I walked through the door.

"What's your name?" the teacher asked. I could hear

agitation in her voice and knew right off that I didn't want to cross her.

"Javier," I replied.

She pointed to a desk near the back row. I made my way over to it and sat down, then looked around. Nobody in the classroom looked familiar. I didn't see one kid from my elementary. It was sad. I took out my notebook and tried to concentrate on what the teacher was saying. Her name was Mrs. McHalenn and she was white. I had to notice because most of the people in my town were Mexicans. The only time I really ever saw white people up close was at school.

Mrs. McHalenn had long blond hair and used her hands a lot when she talked. She started out by telling us the rules for the classroom and what could get you into trouble. She then went on to talk about English and what we were going to do for the semester. She handed out a syllabus and a contract that our parents were supposed to sign. I thought it was funny when a lot of the kids started signing them right then and there. I did the same and slipped the paper into my notebook to turn in the next day. We got two workbooks, a number for our textbook, and a number for our reading book 'cause they were all supposed to stay at school. We also got a copy of *The Call of the Wild.* I'd read it a couple of times before, but I didn't tell Mrs. McHalenn that. It might be better for my grade if she didn't know.

Eventually Mrs. McHalenn gave out our assignment for the period. Some kids worked, others drew pictures on their notebooks, and some, like me, just watched everybody else. I never seemed to get bored just watching people. I had a good way of doing it too. I would prop myself up with a pencil in my hand, like I was doing my assignment, and then I'd just glance around. For this period a couple of the guys were trying to make paper samurai stars, and three girls were trying to talk without getting caught. They would whisper for a while, and then sit straight up at their desks like they were doing their work.

After a while the bell rang. Luckily, I didn't have far to go for my next class—Mrs. McHalenn was my homeroom and reading class teacher too. But I still hadn't decided if I was going to like her or hate her. She was starting out on my negative side, but I had been surprised by teachers before. Some can come off as whack the first week, but they end up being your favorites. I held my decision on Mrs. McHalenn and figured I'd decide in a week or two. Reading was a lot like English. We got another handout to have our parents sign and another syllabus. But then Mrs. McHalenn did the unexpected. Since we were supposed to check out a book a week, she said we were going to tour the library now for our class period. I felt like I'd just won the lottery. I closed up my notebook and jumped in line.

One of the things the eighth-graders didn't have to do that seventh-graders still did was line up. It was kind of embarrassing, like we were still in elementary school or something. A couple of packs of girls started talking and goofing real loud, but girls were like that. They didn't need to know each other all that well to just start talking. Guys were different. If we didn't know each other yet, we weren't going to talk. It wasn't cool, and you'd look like a punk if you just started clowning with somebody you didn't know.

On the way to the library, the line had to stop a couple times for Mrs. McHalenn to put the smackdown on some of the girls, but eventually we made it there. The Orbe Nuevo library was much bigger than the one back at elementary school. There were two floors and books everywhere. The librarian's name was Mrs. Page, and she was like an army sergeant. She laid down the ground rules in full voice after saying that she was the only person in the library that could use a full voice, ever. She went over the procedure for checking out books and how we had to wait at our tables until we were called up to look for our books and check them out. After a while, I got the feeling she actually *had* been in the army. She even made us sit at girl- and guy-only tables.

One of the loud girls stuck her hand up.

"Yes?" Mrs. Page asked.

"That's dumb! Why do we have to sit in girl- and guy-only tables?" the girl asked.

"Because I'm Catholic, and I don't go for any hanky-panky in my library!" Mrs. Page said sternly.

Some of the kids grumbled under their breath and made fun of the words *hanky-panky*. Even I had to chuckle. I decided I was going to like Mrs. Page, not for any other reason but that she took her library seriously. After we found our books, we were supposed to sit at our tables and wait for library cards. Suddenly the glass doors opened and another class came in. They didn't have to wait in line. They were the only classes allowed to come and go to the library when they needed to: special ed.

There were all kinds of special ed classes at Orbe Nuevo. Desi had a brother who was in special ed a few years back, so he knew all about it. There were special ed classes for kids that had trouble learning, and there were special ed classes for kids who had handicaps. They had classes for some who had both. And they had classes for kids who had emotional problems. By the looks of the kids coming through the doors,

22

this must've been a class for the kids that had both learning problems and physical handicaps. A lot of them had helmets on, and two of them were in wheelchairs. A couple of the kids had strange-shaped heads. Their eyes were kind of distant too. One girl had leg braces on and used a walker.

"Whoa! Check out the retards!" a guy at the table behind mine whispered, which made a bunch of kids laugh. "Don't let them touch you or you'll end up retarded!" he added.

Mrs. Page shouted out like a drill instructor, "QUIET DOWN!"

She had a real stern look on her face like she might smack the next kid who said anything. I wouldn't blame her though. Making fun of some special ed kids wasn't exactly cool. It was actually straight-up dumb. But the special ed class didn't seem to notice. Slowly they made their way over to a stack of big picture books. The lady that looked like their teacher started picking up books and showing them to the kids. From what I gathered, she was trying to see which ones made them happy or sad. I guessed the only way she could tell was by their expressions. They probably couldn't speak too well, if at all.

I tried not to look too obvious as I watched them. My mother always said never stare at people like that, but I couldn't help it. Watching people was what I did, and these kids were really interesting to watch. There was this one chubby black kid in a wheelchair. Every time the teacher brought a book up to his face, he'd yell out, "NO! GO AWAY!" The teacher would smile, and then search through the stack of books again. She'd find another and hold it up to his face, and again he'd shout, "NO! GO AWAY!" Again and again the same thing happened.

Then there was another kid. I think I heard the teacher call him Lanzo. I could tell by the way he was looking at a particular book on an upper shelf that he wanted it. The book was blue with glitter on the cover. He couldn't explain that he wanted the book, and I didn't think he could reach for it on his own either. Quietly I got up and tiptoed over to the shelf. When I pulled out the blue book and handed it to him, he smiled but didn't say anything. As I turned around, a booming voice caught me.

"JAVIER!" Mrs. Page called out loudly.

I almost jumped out of my skin. I looked around and the last kid in my class was walking out the door. I'd been so preoccupied that I hadn't even gotten any books to check out. Nervously I walked up to the librarian's desk. She still had a stern look on her face.

"I called your name three times when your class was here. I thought you were absent."

"No. I'm here."

"Books?"

"I didn't get any," I answered, trying to come off innocent.

Mrs. Page sat down at the desk and started typing in my information on the computer. As I waited for her to print out my library card I noticed a box of books by the counter. It looked like a box of donated books. They hadn't even been labeled with library stickers yet. There were random titles, but one caught my eye. Right on top of the stack was a paperback copy of *Islands in the Stream*. The cover had a huge fishing boat on it and a rough-looking man holding a rifle. My eyes shot up to Mrs. Page, who was still busily typing. Then I glanced back down to the box of books. I had to have it. I didn't care that I might get caught. The book looked too good to just leave in the pile. What if Mrs. Page was gonna throw the book out anyway for being too old or something? I'd never find it again.

I took one more glance at her and one around the room. The special ed class was gathering up their stuff to leave. Like a flash, my hand shot down into the box. I grabbed up the book and stuffed it into my belt loop. I was just pulling down my shirt as Mrs. Page finished typing. The book was mine. I had it, and that's all that mattered. I couldn't help but smile as I waited for my card to come out of the printer. When it finally did, I thanked Mrs. Page and said I was sorry to hold her up. She didn't change her expression.

I hustled to the door to catch up with my class, but as I did, the unbelievable happened. As the special ed teacher tried to push the chubby kid's wheelchair through the doorway, my wires got crossed somewhere and I bumped smack into her. No big deal, right? But the *Islands in the Stream* book popped out of my belt loop and fell to the ground. The counter was high enough to hide the evidence from Mrs. Page, but as I went to grab up the book the special ed teacher beat me to it. She held it for a second as she studied the cover, then she looked me over from head to toe. By now Mrs. Page was looking over at us to see what had happened, and I prayed the teacher wouldn't say anything. Once again, she looked at the book, and then she looked at me. Then, strangely, she handed it back to me.

"Thank you for noticing what book Lanzo wanted," the teacher said in a very quiet voice.

I hadn't thought anybody saw when I pulled the book down for that kid.

"No big deal," I said, then barged my way past the special ed kids and down the hall.

To get caught for stealing on the first day of school would've been a mess. I would have gotten a detention. My mom had been in a bad mood for the past couple of weeks, so I knew she would've been all over me. There's one good thing about being poor though. When you're on restriction and lose privileges and stuff, there isn't much that can be taken away from you. It's not like I had all kinds of games for her to hold over my head. I didn't have a computer or a music player or a cell phone. And I pretty much stayed home all the time anyway, so being grounded didn't mean all that much. The only thing my mom could do was tell me not to watch TV, and that was fine with me 'cause we didn't have cable and the only things I really liked to watch were comedy and history shows. But she would have been upset with me for sure, and that would've been enough. When there are only two of you living in a house and the other person isn't talking to you, it sucks pretty bad.

I headed back to my class. When I got there, the kids were already reading their books. The teacher didn't seem to notice I was late, so I just sat down and took out the book I'd swiped. I knew it was going to be good before I even opened it. I would get feelings like that about books. I had that same feeling about *The Red Badge of Courage*, *The Outsiders*, and *The Pigman*. All of them were great. I settled in and started reading, and before I knew it, the bell rang.

Next class was social studies, and it turned out to be pretty cool. Our teacher was an old hippie from the sixties, and he talked in a real hippie way. He even said "groovy" a couple of times, like, "If you need a pencil, young people, the groovy thing to do is just ask me. Don't disturb your neighbors." I thought that was pretty funny.

Since we didn't have our work assignments yet, we stayed in social studies for the next period. We had to fill out cards on what we wanted to do for our jobs. There were three lines for our top three choices. A lot of the girls were going for teacher's aide and office assistant. And a lot of the guys put down PE aide. I couldn't think of anything else I wanted to do, so I put down PE aide on the first two lines so they'd see that that was where I really wanted to go, and then I put down library helper on the third line just in case I didn't get the PE job. We wouldn't find out for a day or two where we were going.

Lunch with Jesse came next, and then I went to math, and then came PE where I got to see Eduardo. By the look on his face, he was having a worse day than me. As we walked onto the field for class I asked him about it.

"This place sucks, man! I already got written up for talking back and being defiant."

"No way, man."

"Desi got busted too. Some eighth-grader didn't know he was one of the Playaz. So this eighth-grader starts talking smack, and Desi's standing behind him, right?"

"Yeah?"

"So Desi hauls off and socks the kid in the dome. He knocks the kid to the ground, and next thing he knows, a security guard is dragging him off to the office. He didn't even make it to fourth period. His mom had to come and pick him up. He's already on suspension."

"No way!"

"Yeah. Some girl we went to elementary school with told me. She saw the whole thing."

"Wow."

"So how's it going for you?"

"Same. I haven't gotten busted yet, so I guess I'm pretty cool."

"Just wait," Eduardo said.

I chuckled.

PE turned out to be all right, especially since I had a friend there. We weren't on the same squad, but every now and then I turned around to check and see what Eduardo was up to, and he'd do the same for me. By the time I made it to science class in the afternoon, I was so tired that it took all my strength just to keep my eyes open. And when the bell finally rang, I felt like I'd just finished running a marathon.

As I walked out the gates I felt sore and my thoughts were all scrambled together. The guys were waiting for me at the curb to walk home, and they looked just as bad as I felt. Desi was there too. After his mom picked him up, he had come back to walk with us. I didn't feel so bad, since everybody had a rough time. If I had been the only one, I would've lied just so I wouldn't come off as a punk. But since we all suffered, we all could whine.

While we were walking home Jesse wasn't the only one who had to go into the bushes to smoke some herb. Eduardo and Desi went with him too. I clutched my backpack and waited for them on the sidewalk. Sure it was a tough day, but I didn't want to get faded over it. Eventually they came out all high and quiet, rubbing their red eyes. We didn't say much to each other after that. I figured we were all thinking the same thing. If it wasn't enough that we just had the hardest day of our lives, we had to go back and do it all over again tomorrow. That thought kept us quiet.

The next day or two were pretty much like the first day. I still got lost going to my classes, and I got confused on where the bathrooms were. Mrs. McHalenn was still tough. Eduardo was having the worst time of his life. The only difference was that on Wednesday we were finding out what we'd get for work experience.

Right after social studies Mr. O'Neil let us have quiet free time again, like we'd had the past couple of days. He was turning out to be a really cool teacher. He taught social studies by telling stories. We hardly ever looked at the book. After the lecture we'd do our work sheets, and when we'd check our answers against the book, all the facts and the people from the stories were there, where they should be.

During quiet free time I read *Islands in the Stream*. It was turning out to be a great book. I was so into it that I didn't notice the office secretary come into our room. I looked up to see her hand a stack of cards to Mr. O'Neil and leave. As Mr. O'Neil looked over the cards one by one, everybody stopped what they were doing. After a while he cleared his throat.

"I have your work assignments here, so when I call your name, please come up and get your card. And look, young people, don't get wild and crazy when you find out where you're going. If you have a legitimate excuse to not do the job you're assigned, just bring a note in tomorrow. Okay. Here goes."

Mr. O'Neil started calling us up. Each kid would either get all happy or look sad. It seemed like a lot of people were going where they wanted to 'cause a lot of scared faces changed to happy ones after looking at the cards. I noticed a lot of the guys were getting PE aide. Too many were. That was bad for me. How many PE aides could they need? As I waited, I settled in with the idea that I was going to the library. Like her or not, Mrs. Page and I were going to be working together. I mean, there were much, much worse places to go, right?

"Javier?" Mr. O'Neil called out.

Coolly, I got up from my desk and went up to the front of the room. Mr. O'Neil had a strange smile on his face as he glanced at my card. I wondered what that was about. When I reached him, he handed me the card, and then said, "Here you go, buddy. You're going to be all right."

I said thank you but was puzzled. What was he talking about? Was I going off to war or something? I figured he meant Mrs. Page. Working for her would be like going into the army. When I got back to my desk, I finally glanced down and saw the assignment.

Over and over again, I looked at the card to see if the words would suddenly change. I even closed my eyes and opened them a couple of times, but the words still said the same thing: Aide, special ed—physically disabled.

I swallowed hard and prayed that it was just a bad dream.

# CHAPTER 3

"SPECIAL ED!" Eduardo cried out as he read my work assignment card.

As we stood on the sidewalk on our way home from school, all the guys gathered around to look at the card in Eduardo's hands, just to see it for themselves. I'd wondered if it was a good idea even to show them what assignment I'd gotten 'cause they had all gotten the ones they wanted. Eduardo and Desi both got PE aide, and Jesse got computer lab assistant.

"Physically disabled, even! No way!" Jesse spoke up.

"Oh, man. That sucks!" Desi said.

"I know. I don't know how it happened. I put down PE twice, and then the library after that," I pleaded.

"THE LIBRARY!" Eduardo shrieked.

I'd forgotten that libraries weren't cool with the guys and had to cover up real fast.

"Just in case I didn't get PE, I didn't want to wind up scraping gum off desks or something."

"Oh," Eduardo said sympathetically. "But still, man, special ed? You gotta get this changed."

"I know. I'm trying to work that out."

"If people find out you've got special ed, you're going to hear it for the rest of your life," Desi explained.

"They're going to start calling you retard," Jesse said.

"Yeah. Mr. Retardo and stuff," Desi added.

Eduardo started lisping really badly and talking in a monotone voice like he was deaf. "Ja-Vier! Did youu sayyy some-thinggg?"

"Cut it out, man!" I said.

"Just giving you a taste of what it's going to be like," Eduardo said.

"I know. But it's not funny. It's really going to happen."

Just hearing the guys was already making me scared of what the rest of the school might say if they knew I was working in the special ed class. The guys knew how kids thought, and I knew too. They wouldn't see it like I was just doing my job. They'd see it like I was special ed too, that I was a part of the class with the rest of them. I'd be done as far as middle school went. They'd start calling me names nonstop. It wouldn't matter that I was one of the Southside Playaz. I could whup the whole school, but the next day I'd still be Mr. Retardo.

When the guys slipped into the bushes for some herb, I seriously thought about going with them this time. I didn't want to feel what I was going through. How could something be so messed up? I looked down at my new shoes and wondered if it was bad luck for all the things I'd stolen. Maybe this is how it was all coming back to me for taking so many things that weren't mine.

When I got home that day, my mom was already at work. All I could do was read and try to forget the mess. It wasn't going to get any better if I worried about it. I'd just go to the office in the morning and have my assignment changed. That's all I had to do.

The next day before the first bell rang, I went straight to

the administration office. It was the first time I'd been in there. Like everything at Orbe Nuevo, it was huge. Back at elementary there was one secretary at a desk in front of the principal's office, but Orbe Nuevo's was like a regular office building. There were desks everywhere, with four or five secretaries hustling around. There were parents waiting and a line of kids already sitting in the detention chairs. The school day hadn't even started yet and some kids were already in trouble. In the hustle I spotted the secretary that brought over our assignment cards the day before. She had a cubicle behind the long counter that blocked off the office from the visitors. I think she was the lead secretary 'cause her desk had a little shelf around it with family pictures and plants and stuff. I held up my card at her. She spotted me and buzzed the swinging door that led to behind the counter.

As I walked through the door I saw a guy that I guessed was the principal having a talk with some parents. They weren't Desi's parents, but I thought of them 'cause it sounded like the principal was explaining why their kid was put on suspension already. The parents could hardly speak English, and the principal didn't seem to know a word of Spanish. By the looks of the office, he was going to have a really long day.

"Yes?" the secretary asked me when I got to her desk.

"I need another assignment," I said, dropping my card in front of her.

She picked up the card and looked it over for a few seconds.

"Sure," she said. Then she went into her desk for another card.

Wow, I thought. This was going to be easy. And here I'd stressed out about it almost a day already for no reason.

After pawing through her desk, the secretary pulled out

33

three different forms and a new blank assignment card. As I watched her fill out a form I started to feel much better about everything. Then, from out of nowhere, she asked, "And what's your legitimate excuse?"

"Huh?"

"Your excuse? To have your assignment changed, you need a legitimate excuse."

She held her pen close to the paper, waiting for me to say something. My mind went blank.

"What's that?" I asked, to give myself time to think.

"A legitimate excuse is something like a medical condition or a class-scheduling conflict that would preclude you from doing your assignment. Are you diabetic and need to get your insulin shot at that time?"

"No."

"Are you a high achiever and wish to have a study-specific assignment?"

"No."

"And you're not physically disabled?"

"No."

"Then what's your excuse?"

This was going all wrong! She had me trapped. There wasn't any real reason why I couldn't work with the special ed class.

"I-I-I can't" fell out of my mouth.

"You can't?"

Just remembering what I'd heard some kids say in PE, I blurted out, "I have asthma!"

The secretary rolled her eyes and gently ripped the forms down the middle. She handed my original work assignment card back to me.

"Bye, Javier. Have a nice workday with Mrs. Aronson's class."

"Shit," I mumbled under my breath, and took the card back.

Beaten, I dragged myself to first period. The situation was impossible. There was no way to change it.

For the first three periods of the day, I was in a trance. It was like I couldn't hear or feel anything, like I knew I was going to die in three hours and I was just counting down the minutes. I got called on twice in Mrs. McHalenn's classes, and then Mr. O'Neil called on me in social studies, but I couldn't even put a sentence together, let alone the answers they wanted. I looked like a total dweeb, and everybody saw. It was just a glimpse of what my life was going to be like once they all found out I worked in special ed.

Right before work experience period, I went to the longest line I could find for a drink of water. Then I went to the bathroom clear across on the other side of campus, the farthest bathroom from the portables where the special ed classes were. I stayed in there past the bell, knowing that I could get marked tardy or absent. I thought about ditching my work period altogether. I could wait it out in the bathroom, and when the bell rang, go off to lunch. Sure, I'd get an absence for the day, but that was better than having to live down the shame of being Mr. Retardo. Standing at a sink, I turned the water on and just let it run. I watched the stream hit the basin and flow down the drain. I wished that I was that water, that I could simply disappear down the drain too. Then all of sudden, WHOOSH! The bathroom door was flung open. It was a security guard.

"Y'ALL ARE TARDY FOR CLASS! LET'S GO!" the security guard shouted out in a booming voice, even though I was the only person in the bathroom. I couldn't escape now. I grabbed my backpack, and the security guard walked me all the way across campus. He even wrote out a tardy slip while we were walking.

"Ah, come on, man! I was using the bathroom!" I pleaded.

"Y'all have plenty of time for that during pass period."

"But I really had to go!"

"Whatever."

"That's messed up, man!"

"Whatever."

When we got to the classroom, I thought I might have a chance to make a break for it. I could still ditch when we reached the classroom and the guard turned around to leave. I could hit the fences and jam over to the wash, then hide there until I figured out what I was going to do. But the security guard must have read my mind because he didn't just drop me off at my classroom, he walked me inside too. They only did that for kids who were real trouble.

With a big smile he went straight over to my work experience teacher's desk.

"How ya doin', Mrs. Aronson? Caught me a ditcher," he said, then handed her my tardy slip.

"Thank you, Mr. Jackson."

"Y'all have a nice day," he said. Then he left.

Standing there in front of Mrs. Aronson's desk, I didn't know what to do. I was scared to turn around and look at her students even though I heard them from over my shoulder. From behind me the chubby black kid I'd seen at the library a couple days back yelled out, "NO! GO AWAY!"

Mrs. Aronson's classroom was bigger than most, and there was all kinds of strange stuff to look at. There was even a kitchen with a fridge, a stove, and ovens and everything. I didn't want Mrs. Aronson to notice me staring, so I kept my eyes on the ceiling.

Sitting behind a pile of paperwork on her desk, Mrs. Aronson slid her glasses up her nose to look me over. She seemed about my mom's age. Her hair was dark brown and frizzy, and she had tons of it. She was smart looking, like she was smart about everything, not just smart in her classroom. And she spoke softly, so softly I could barely hear what she was saying.

"So you had trouble finding my class?"

I broke my gaze from the ceiling to look Mrs. Aronson right in the eye. "I really had to go to the bathroom."

"Well, that's understandable," she said. Then she balled up the tardy slip and threw it into the trash can beside her desk. I was shocked.

"You're not going to turn that in?"

"Oh, I figured you might have a little trouble finding the classroom on your first day. As long as it doesn't happen again, I don't think I have to worry about that one."

I didn't know if I should say thanks or what, so I didn't say anything. Mrs. Aronson sifted through some of the paperwork in front of her to find a file with my name on it. She read something inside, and then she looked up at me.

"So you want to be a PE aide?"

Shocked that she knew, I replied, "Yeah! I don't know what happened."

"We do PE," Mrs. Aronson said simply, then leaned back far in her chair.

"I meant *real* PE."

"We do *real* PE here."

I wanted to say more, but it wouldn't have been nice. And I

knew better than that. Mrs. Aronson must have known she had me beat 'cause she tilted her head and smiled.

"Javier, let me show you around," she said, getting up from her desk.

I gave in, for now.

"You can put your backpack down. You're here for fifty minutes."

I kept my backpack on in hopes that I'd be out the door faster. Sighing and shaking my head, I followed her across the room. There were maybe ten kids in class, the same kids I'd seen at the library a couple of days back. There was a teacher's aide too, an older lady named Mrs. Rogers. Each student had a half-moon-shaped desk with all kind of things on it. They had pencils and crayons and blocks. There were strange things too, like strips of fabric and pieces of fake grass. There were huge cutouts of pennies and dimes and quarters. And each kid had a CD player with earphones.

Mrs. Aronson started naming off the kids. She'd stop at one desk and introduce me, then go on to the next. She said it was reading time, so the class had their assignments to do. I didn't know that they actually got real assignments, but they did. Each kid had a work sheet to do on a book they were reading. A few didn't look like they could read, since they just kept turning the pages. Some of the kids had ABC books with lots of colorful pictures. At each kid's desk Mrs. Aronson would stop and look over their work sheets. Then she'd coach them to keep going.

"All right, Lanzo!" she said as she stopped at the desk of a kid whose head was shaped a little strangely. "You're doing great. Don't stop. Keep going. I know you can finish that before the end of reading."

I looked down at Lanzo's work sheet. He could barely write a word that was readable.

As we left his desk Mrs. Aronson explained that Lanzo was still learning how to hold a pencil. It had taken him years to just get to that point, and he couldn't even hold it that well. I couldn't believe it. I started to feel sad. I'd learned how to hold a pencil back in kindergarten, and this guy was in middle school and couldn't do it. I didn't want to say the wrong thing, so I just nodded.

The next kid was Joe. He kept flipping the pages of his book, and then when he got to the end, he'd start back up on the first page. Over and over again he did this while Mrs. Aronson was checking in on him. And once again she coached.

"Joe, take your time. Look at each page before turning it. Let's see if we can notice anything different in the pictures from one page to the next."

"NO! GO AWAY!" I heard behind me again. My head spun around, and the chubby kid in the wheelchair was pushing away another book as the aide was trying to show it to him.

I went on with Mrs. Aronson from desk to desk. Each desk made me feel worse than the last. I started to feel guilty about not wanting to show up. These kids actually needed help . . . with everything. My reasons for not wanting to be there were starting to feel pretty dumb.

The last student I met was the wheelchair kid. When I first saw him in the library, he had been wearing his helmet, so I couldn't really see his face. But now I noticed that he was black and had puffy hair. He smirked the whole time, like nothing pleased him. His name was Dontae.

Dontae looked Mrs. Aronson squarely in the eyes and said loudly, "NO! GO AWAY!"

Mrs. Aronson took me aside and explained that the phrase was Dontae's echolalia response for just about everything. It was functional and nonfunctional, which meant he would say it if he was happy or sad or hungry or thirsty. He would say it if he liked something or didn't like something. But sometimes he'd say it just to say it and not mean or want anything.

"Once you get to know him a little, you'll know what he wants and what he means by the *way* he says it," Mrs. Aronson said.

Then she turned to Dontae and asked, "Well, maybe there are just too many people in your face, Dontae? Is that what it is? How about Mrs. Rogers and I give you some space, and we'll let Javier work with you for a while? How does that sound?"

"NO! GO AWAY!"

The teacher's aide got up from her chair across from Dontae and went off with Mrs. Aronson. I was alone with him. For a second or two we just stared at each other. In truth, I was scared. I wasn't scared that he might try to hit me or something; I was scared that I might upset him. Slowly I took off my backpack and laid it under the desk. Then I sat down and noticed the box of books on the floor beside him. I picked up the book on top. It was an Amelia Bedelia book. I'd loved those when I was in the second or third grade. I hoped he'd like to hear it so I could read it again, but when I brought it up into his eyes, he sounded off.

"NO! GO AWAY!"

I put the book down and grabbed for another one. And once again Dontae yelled out.

"NO! GO AWAY!"

Again and again the same thing happened. There must have been a good fifteen to twenty books in that box, and for every one Dontae had the same response: "NO! GO AWAY!"

Frustrated, I didn't know what to do.

"Take a deep breath, Javier," Mrs. Aronson said to me from across the room. I guess she'd been watching my progress, or lack of it. "There's no race. Patience is your best friend."

I started to feel like the special ed kid when she said that. I looked around Dontae's desk, but there weren't any more books to show him. I thought I'd try to help him draw a picture, but I couldn't find any paper on the desk. Grabbing up my backpack, I opened it up and started pulling things out to find my notebook.

"READ!" Dontae yelled.

I almost jumped out of my skin. Even Mrs. Aronson and the aide stopped what they were doing, wide-eyed.

Again he called out, "READ!"

I looked all around to see what he was talking about.

"READ!"

"What?" I asked him.

"READ!"

He was looking toward my hand. I was holding a mess of stuff. There was a notepad, a bunch of work sheets, and a workbook from English that I wasn't supposed to take home but did anyway.

"This?" I asked him, puzzled that he'd want me to read out of my workbook.

"READ!" he said again.

Then I caught a glimpse of something else. The cover of *Islands in the Stream* was peaking out from all the things I was holding. When I held it up to him, he looked directly at the cover.

"READ!"

That was it. He wanted me to read out of the book. I turned

around to check with Mrs. Aronson, and she nodded her head urgently.

"All right, Dontae," I said. "Here goes."

I opened the book and went to the page I had stopped on the night before, figuring he wouldn't know the difference. I cleared my throat and began.

"READ!" Dontae interrupted.

"I am," I said.

"READ!"

I looked at Mrs. Aronson again for help.

"I believe he'd like you to start on the first page, Javier."

"Why? He knows this book?"

"No. I don't think so. But he does know when you're starting from the beginning of a book."

Surprised, I went back to the first page.

This time Dontae didn't say anything. As I read the first paragraph about a house in Bimini, his mouth fell open, then his eyes closed. Slowly he began rocking back and forth, like he was going into a trance or something. Without stopping my reading, I glanced over at Mrs. Aronson.

With a smile she mouthed, "He likes it," then she gave me a thumbs-up.

I shrugged and kept reading.

Dontae didn't stop listening. He went on rocking with his eyes closed and mouth open. Page after page, I wondered if he understood what he was hearing. I couldn't figure out why he'd want to hear *Islands in the Stream* and not an early reader or something. Pretty soon, I got caught up in the story and forgot I was reading for him. We must've done ten pages, and I probably wouldn't have stopped if Mrs. Aronson hadn't spoke up.

"All right. We've got just enough time for a short PE."

My mouth was dry and my eyes were tired. I was ready for a break, but I guess Dontae wasn't.

"READ!" he called out with his eyes closed.

"Ahhh," Mrs. Aronson sang. "Dontae's found a story he likes!"

"READ!" Dontae repeated.

"We'll have to wait until Javier comes again tomorrow, Dontae. Right now we've got PE. Okay, everyone. Let's get our helmets on."

Mrs. Aronson and the aide began to help the other students get ready. I wondered what kind of PE they could possibly do. As I was putting away my book Mrs. Aronson brought over Dontae's helmet.

"Javier, do you mind?" Mrs. Aronson said as she handed me Dontae's helmet.

"No, I got it."

After helping Dontae, I grabbed a hold of the handles on his wheelchair and we followed the others outside. Suddenly, I was worried about people seeing me with the special ed class. Pretty soon the rest of the kids would know. I was about to be officially titled Mr. Retardo.

I thought about making up some dumb excuse to just get away. Maybe I could fake sick or say I had to see the counselor or something. Right before we passed through the doorway, I looked down at Dontae. He didn't seem to be bothered by anything. He had that smirk on his face, but he looked happy that we were going outside. What could I do? I couldn't just leave him there.

So outside we went. My only chance at going unnoticed was if, and only if, nobody saw us. We were heading to the blacktop in front of the soccer field and were only a few yards out of the classroom when the first lunch bell suddenly rang. I couldn't believe it. If we'd only left five minutes sooner! In a matter of seconds, a third of the school was going to be out of their classes, and any kind of cool I thought I had was about to be blown.

Quickly doors were flung open as kids left their classes. They were eighth-graders mostly, since they had first lunch. Mrs. Aronson's line was moving slowly because she was guiding the girl with leg braces. They were at the front of the line, and I was bringing up the rear with Dontae. I looked straight down at him, just waiting. I knew it was coming . . . and then it happened.

"Javier!" a kid called out.

I didn't want to look up. I didn't want to turn around. Maybe I could pretend I didn't hear it and he'd go away.

"JAVIER!" the kid called out louder.

I had to look up. He'd keep yelling if I didn't, and that would bring even more attention to me. Reluctantly I raised my head and looked in the direction of the voice. When I saw who it was, I wished not only that I had ditched that day of school but that I had ditched being born altogether. The kid yelling was Enrique, an eighth-grader I'd gone to elementary school with. He'd been in sixth grade when I was in fifth. He was a member of the Playaz, and he was also the most trash-talking kid I'd ever known in my life. He wouldn't just make fun of your mom or your clothes, he'd make fun of your whole existence as a person. And now he was on my case. I kept pushing Dontae.

"What's up, man?" I called back to him.

Enrique's eyes were sparkling. He was downright aching to start talking trash. It was a miracle he'd held out this long already.

"What are you doing? Are you in that class?" he asked.

"I'm helping," I said.

"What? The retards?" Enrique cried out with a chuckle.

Then like a flash, Mrs. Aronson spun around with the hardest look I'd ever seen on a teacher in my life.

"ENRIQUE! OFFICE! NOW!" she commanded.

Dumbfounded, Enrique held up his hands.

"What I do?"

"You know exactly what you did. Don't make me have to walk you over there!" Mrs. Aronson added.

"What I do? Ah, man, that's messed up!"

Enrique turned around and started toward the office. When Mrs. Aronson saw that he was well on his way, she continued on with the girl in leg braces. *Never judge a book by its cover*, I thought as I went on pushing Dontae, 'cause nothing would have ever made me think that Mrs. Aronson could be hard-core. I got the feeling that she might be the nicest person in the world, but if you messed with her kids, you'd get it.

The special ed PE class was way different from any PE class I'd ever had. To begin with, the kids got in a big circle. Those who could stand did, and the rest sat in their wheelchairs. The class started out with clapping and arm-raising exercises. When Mrs. Aronson caught me standing around just watching, she yelled out with a smile, "Let's get with it, Javier! You wanted to be a PE aide!" Grumbling, I took off my backpack and started to do the exercises with the kids.

Mrs. Aronson had everyone stretch to the sky, then try to touch their toes. Then she broke out a boom box and played a CD that had clapping exercises on it. After we did that for like five minutes, she took out a ball, and we passed it around the circle and bounced it to different people. I spent most of the time trying to show Dontae how to catch the ball, but every time it came to him, he'd fumble it. It wasn't something that I could teach him just like that. It would take some practice, but I bet I could help him catch the ball eventually.

It turned out to be kind of fun having PE with Mrs. Aronson's class. I ran all over the place after the ball when it bounced out of the circle. And every time it was Dontae's turn, he'd get this big old happy smile on his face. He'd throw the ball and then clap his hands. He was having a great time. Then all of a sudden my lunch bell rang. I could never admit it, but I didn't want to go. I felt like I was actually doing something important.

"We'll see you tomorrow, Javier," Mrs. Aronson said, putting the ball away.

"You need help getting Dontae back to class?" I asked, putting on my backpack.

"No. We have it, Javier. We'll see you tomorrow."

That afternoon as I walked home with the guys I didn't mention anything about what happened to me that day. I knew they wouldn't understand. In truth, I didn't understand it. But ever since Mrs. Aronson's class, I'd felt lighter inside, kind of happy. It was one of the best feelings that I'd ever felt in my life, and I couldn't tell anybody. The guys didn't seem to notice at all. There were a couple of girls walking ahead of us, and Eduardo was busy clowning for them. Every now and then the girls would turn around and smile, and that just made him bolder. Jesse and Desi were laughing like crazy.

As we walked along, a fly black street racer pulled up alongside us. It had twenty-inch rims and a booming system. Roberto was behind the wheel. He was only fifteen, and he couldn't even have a license, let alone his own car, but there he was. The guys quit clowning and broke out cool all of a sudden. Roberto handled some business for the Playaz, so when he came around, the guys would always make like they were serious. Roberto had gone to school with us, but he was a couple of years ahead. The trouble he'd gotten into in elementary school was legendary. He got caught smoking herb in the bathroom in the fifth grade. He cursed out just about every teacher he'd ever had. He'd been to juvie and YA. But now he was out.

Roberto didn't care about getting into trouble. He liked the reputation of being loco. It made people scared of him, including me. I never knew what to say when he was around or how to act. I never wanted anything I did to seem like a challenge, so I wouldn't do anything when I was around him. But the rest of the guys would be in awe when he came by, especially Eduardo.

"Cherry ride!" Eduardo wailed when he saw who was behind the wheel.

"What's up?" Roberto replied.

The guys crowded around the car and started poking their heads into the windows and stuff. I did the same, but I didn't get too close to him.

"Where you going?" Desi asked.

"Across town. I've got to drop off something for the crew. You rolling? I could use backup."

Eduardo and Desi stumbled all over themselves to climb into the car. I didn't have an excuse not to go, but I didn't want to roll with them. To be honest, I wanted to go home and eat and read my book. But I couldn't say that without sounding like a nerd.

"What's up with you, Javier?" Roberto asked.

"My mom's waiting for me. I have to go to the dentist."

"Shit," Roberto muttered.

He didn't bother asking Jesse what his excuse was because even he knew Jesse had his church classes in the afternoon, and that his parents would probably send out a search party if he wasn't home on time.

"All right. Peace out," Roberto said, and sped off.

Jesse and I watched them round a corner, then roll out of sight.

"What do you think he's up to?" I asked Jesse.

"No good!" he shot back with a chuckle.

# CHAPTER 4

Jesse had been right. My mom was still at work when I got home, so I was halfway through *Islands in the Stream* when the phone rang. It was Eduardo's mom talking real nervously in Spanish. She spoke way too fast, and I had to tell her to slow down and repeat herself a couple of times before I started to understand her. The gist of it was that it was eight o'clock and Eduardo hadn't come home yet. He hadn't called or anything. I couldn't rat out my homeboy, so I said I didn't know where he was. And I most definitely didn't tell her that he'd gotten into a car with Roberto and they'd headed off for the other side of town. All the parents knew Roberto was trouble; she would've had a heart attack if I'd told her the truth. I wasn't too worried about the guys anyway. The way I saw it, they were probably gaming at some *vato*'s house and just lost track of time. I never could've imagined the trouble they were actually in.

I found out the whole story the next morning on my way to school. I walked with Jesse, and he could barely control himself. He even had to get high on the way so he could calm down enough to tell me. Right after Eduardo's mom called me, she called Jesse's house. He didn't rat either, but he lives next door to Eduardo, so he waited in his backyard until Eduardo got home, which wasn't until eleven o'clock. Eduardo showed up on foot, looking like he'd been in one crazy fight. His lips were split and all puffy. He had smears of blood on his shirt, and his knuckles were all raw.

The guys had run into some serious trouble on the other side of town. Eduardo had said to Jesse that it all started out cool. They rolled across town and Roberto dropped off the package for the Playaz, getting the money he was supposed to get. Then they'd hung out with those vatos for a while, drinking beer and gaming until about seven thirty. On their way back home, they spotted a DUI checkpoint. Not wanting to get busted, Roberto ditched his car in an alley behind his cousin's house, and from there they started walking. It was at least five miles back to our neighborhood, but they were making pretty good time. Then they ran into a snag.

They were on Canyon Avenue, and just a mile or two into their walk, when a couple of kids walked up to them and asked what set they claimed. Roberto told them straight up, "Southside Playaz." The kids walked off like nothing, and he and the guys went on their way. But by the time they made it to the end of the block, there were four high school dudes plus the two kids from before waiting for them. It was a dark street, and the guys didn't know where to go. There was no place to run. Wherever they went, they'd be in the same barrio, some-one else's hood. So it was on.

From what Eduardo told Jesse, Roberto was fearless. He didn't care that they were outnumbered; he just dived in and started swinging, keeping three high schoolers busy for a good minute and a half while Desi and Eduardo tried to handle the rest. Eduardo said he could barely see. It was that dark. He just kept hitting and swinging, and when he felt someone behind him, he'd elbow.

Then all of a sudden, Roberto yelled out, "Haul ass, guys!" and they ran off down the street. Eduardo said he looked behind him once, when they were twenty yards or so away. The other kids were hunched over, whupped breathless. Eduardo told Jesse they must have run a good mile before slowing down to a walk. And from there they came home.

"Whatever Roberto had to drop off must have been really important," Jesse added.

"Why?" I asked.

" 'Cause he gave Eduardo and Desi forty bucks apiece!"

"No way!"

"Eduardo said Roberto didn't even trip over it. He gave it to them like it was nothing. That dude's got mad *dinero*!"

"Shit." I sighed, wondering how I could have turned them down. Forty bucks! With that kind of money, I could've paid for my shoes in cash.

Jesse told me that Eduardo and Desi weren't coming to school that day. They were too sore and bruised up from the night before. By the time they'd gotten home, their parents were so relieved they were okay that they didn't trip out on them. The guys had lied and told their folks they were gaming at a friend's house close-by when they got jumped by some high schoolers. So it had all worked out for them, and they got the money in the end. I wondered if I would've been able to get away with it. Actually, the night before, my mom had gotten home from work at eleven fifteen. I would've made it back and had fifteen minutes to get cleaned up and settled in like I hadn't been anywhere at all.

"No," Jesse said out of the blue.

"No, what?"

"You wouldn't have gotten away with it."

I guess Jesse had figured out what I was thinking. "Why not?"

"It's not your luck. Remember the other day when you told us the security guard found you hiding in the bathroom? And remember when Enrique caught you with the special ed class? And that says a lot right there. Why did you got the special ed class when we all got the jobs we wanted? Your luck is different. You would've got caught."

Jesse was smart in a lot of ways. He was probably right.

Amused, Jesse smiled, and then said, "Sorry, vato, but you're like Jonah."

"Jonah?"

"You know, like from the Bible. Jonah and the whale."

"How?"

"God pays too much attention to you. When you do something wrong, he makes your life miserable."

"Yeah, but why me?"

Jesse shrugged. "Maybe he wants you to do something for him."

"Like what?"

"I don't know. But it sure isn't getting forty bucks from Roberto!"

"Shit." I sighed as Jesse started to laugh. He laughed so hard, he started to cough. He'd been smoking so much herb since school started that for the past few days he'd begun to have coughing fits. For such a smart guy, I wondered why he had to get high all the time. He sure did strike a nerve with me though. All that stuff about God paying too much attention made me think he had something there.

When we got to school, I kept thinking about Mrs. Aronson's

class. As I sat in English trying to avoid doing my work I wondered if Dontae would want me to keep reading from the same book when I saw him later. I'd already read over half of *Islands in the Stream*, but there were parts I wanted to read over again, so I didn't mind.

I sat in Mrs. McHalenn's class and daydreamed. Just in case she looked over at me, I had my workbook open and a pencil on a page, but that was as much as I was doing. I just couldn't stop wondering how Dontae might see the world. Was it different from how the rest of us saw it? Maybe it was like a cartoon to him or something. Maybe that's why he reacted the way he did.

"JAVIER! Three pages are due at the end of class. They're your ticket out the door. You had better get them done," Mrs. McHalenn said loudly from across the room.

I guess I hadn't looked busy enough. I could feel the eyes of the other kids on me, so I kept my eyes on my workbook and didn't look up. But after a few moments passed, I started thinking about Dontae again. It would suck to not walk. I mean sure, my life sucked, but it would suck even worse if I had to be in that chair all day! I'd have to ask for somebody's help for everything. I couldn't shoot hoops with the guys, or walk home from school, which was one of my favorite times of the day. No wonder Dontae always said, "No. Go away!" I'd be bent too if I were like that. As I thought about that, the bell suddenly rang.

I'd heard that line about class work being my "ticket out the door" more than a few times back in elementary school. If I played by the rules, I'd have to show my work to leave the room. But I didn't feel like playing by the rules that day. I stuffed my work in my backpack and waited. Just like always, a swarm of kids surrounded Mrs. McHalenn's desk when class ended. So when a group of girls walked out the door, I shadowed them out. As I passed through the doorway I heard behind me, "Javier!"

I'd made it. I was free, and I wouldn't have to see Mrs. McHalenn until tomorrow. I'd have time to regroup by then, and maybe even try to get the work done that had been due today. I was wading through tons of people on my way to Mr. O'Neil's class when, from out of nowhere, someone shoved my back and I stumbled into four or five kids. Angrily I turned around and came face-to-face with Enrique.

"What's up with that?" I cried out.

"You got me busted! I gotta do a week of detention for you, punk!"

"What I do?"

"It was you and your dumb retard class, bitch!"

"You better step off, punk! Unless you're ready to throw down!" I yelled.

It was all talk. There was no way I could risk looking weak in front of the whole school, even though I knew there wouldn't be a fight. Enrique knew it was all talk too 'cause we were both Southside Playaz, from the same set and the same neighborhood. And even though we weren't really friends or anything, on the street and in our clique we were brothers. And for one of the Playaz to throw down with another, there had to be a meeting and it had to be approved, or we could both get whupped bad by the other Playaz for getting out of line. And neither one of us would ever bring up something as stupid as this to the other homeboys. So trash talk was as far as it was going to go.

"You better check yourself! Retard!" Enrique said. Then he walked off.

"Dumb-ass," I muttered.

I made my way through the kids who were already standing around waiting for a fight and went on to Mr. O'Neil's room.

Social studies was turning out to be one of my favorite classes. I was right in thinking the teacher was a hippie 'cause every now and then he'd talk about some protest or march that he had been a part of. He'd marched for civil rights back in the sixties. And he'd sat in for the farmworkers up north with Cesar Chavez. He had pictures of Jim Morrison, Jimi Hendrix, and Janis Joplin on his wall with their ages and the dates they died and a caption that read: DON'T LET THIS HAPPEN TO YOU. And the way he taught made it seem like we weren't in class at all. We started out the semester with ancient civilizations like the Nile River and Indus River cultures, and he would talk about them like they were people who lived in the next city or something. He'd explain what they ate and how different that is from what we eat now, and why they were successful cultures, and how we all come from those ancient peoples in one way or another. "We're all the products of successful genetic strains," he said. When the bell rang at the end of class, it caught me by surprise. It felt like fifteen minutes had gone by, the whole time I was there.

As I walked toward the portable classrooms I thought about the day before, when I would have done just about anything to avoid Mrs. Aronson's class. Today I wasn't as scared that people might see me, but I kept my head down just in case and focused on the work I had to do. Actually, I was really looking forward to reading to Dontae again. I liked knowing that I was doing something important.

Life's weird like that. The things we think we might hate the most sometimes turn out to be things we like the best.

But once I got inside the classroom, I was caught off guard.

"Dontae's absent today. He has a doctor's appointment. You'll be helping Nena, Javier," Mrs. Aronson said as she pointed to a girl's desk.

Nena was the girl who wore leg braces and used the walker. She was Mexican, and because of her condition, I guessed, she hadn't grown that tall. She was like half my height. She also had really thick glasses that were strapped to her head.

"Here you go," Mrs. Aronson said as she dropped two huge books into my hands.

I took the books and made my way to Nena's desk. *This is strange*, I thought. I kind of knew what to expect with Dontae, but with Nena, I didn't have a clue. When I got to her desk, I didn't look at her at first. I just dropped my backpack down and put her books on the table. Figuring I better say something, I mumbled out "hi" under my breath.

"Nena doesn't communicate that way," Mrs. Aronson said from across the room.

I turned to look to Mrs. Aronson, not sure of what she meant.

"You might do better if you said it this way," Mrs. Aronson explained. Then she held her hand flat up to her cheek and waved off sharply.

"Huh?" I said.

"It's sign language. It means 'hi.'"

"Oh."

I turned to Nena just as she looked up from the work sheet she had in front of her. Her glasses were really thick. As I tried to look through them, it was like trying to see through blurry marble. Her eyes looked small and weak, like they could barely make out anything. I made my hand flat like I'd seen Mrs. Aronson do, held it up to my cheek, and waved off sharply.

"Hi," I said.

Nena smiled big and did the same greeting. I sat down and picked up one of the books Mrs. Aronson had handed to me. Opening it up, I was surprised to see plastic pages. On them were raised shapes like coffee cups and spoons and forks and all kinds of things.

"What the . . . ?" I said as I looked at the shapes.

Nena was squinting at her work sheet. I glanced back at the book to try to make sense of it. It was like a Braille book, but instead of dots with letters and punctuation and stuff, it was filled with objects to touch.

"Getting started?" Mrs. Aronson asked, coming up behind me.

"What is this?" I replied, pointing to the book.

"It's a book of tangible symbols."

"What's it for?"

"Well, first off, Nena's hard of hearing, and unfortunately, her eyes are getting weaker. If they continue to get weaker, she may not be able to see and she'll have trouble communicating what she wants. So Nena is beginning to learn Braille as well as tangible symbols. See the shape of the potato?"

"Yeah."

"Well, when Nena wants a potato but can't say that, she'll show us she wants one by feeling for this shape and making its sign."

Mrs. Aronson turned the page over. There was a picture of a hot, buttery baked potato on it.

"Now, on the back we have a picture that Nena can associate the shape with. That way she'll be able to point to the picture for now and know the shape later when her eyes get weaker."

"Ohhh," I said. "I get it."

"So you quiz her on what she likes. Show her the picture on the back first. Then let her feel the shape. Then ask her if she likes what it is she's seeing and feeling."

"How do I do that?"

Mrs. Aronson showed me the signs, and I almost started to laugh. It looked like she was throwing down gang signs.

"What's so funny?"

I guess I must've been smiling. "Nothing," I said, shaking my head.

It took me a minute or two to get it down, but once I had the signs for *do*, *you*, and *like*, I was ready. I turned to Nena, who was still scribbling, and waved my hand. Then I said "hi" again to her in sign, and she said "hi" back. I pointed to the book, and she nodded her head like she understood what we were going to do. There was a shape of a piece of cake on the first page. I turned the page to show Nena the picture, and once again she nodded her head like she understood. Then slowly I went through the signs, asking her if she liked cake.

Nena smiled and made a sign like she was revving up a motorcycle. I didn't know what it meant, so I turned around to ask Mrs. Aronson.

"It means 'yes,' " she replied.

"Oh. And what's 'no'?"

Mrs. Aronson made a sign with three fingers like a duck's bill closing.

And from that point on, Nena and I worked. I learned a lot about her. I learned that she liked sweets but not vegetables. She also liked cats and horses and French fries. She got real happy when she felt the pieces of candy, and she also grew a big smile when she felt the shape of a doll. When we got to the test page in the back of the book, she picked out most of the things she liked by their shapes, without having to look at the pictures. So I figured it was a good lesson.

"Time for PE," Mrs. Aronson called out.

I put the books away and helped Nena get her walker, and then we made our way to the door. It kind of surprised me, but I wasn't all that worried about being seen with Mrs. Aronson's class this time around. Little by little I was getting cooler with the whole idea of working with them.

When we got out to the blacktop for PE, I had to grin when Mrs. Aronson pulled out a ball and a miniature basketball hoop from the PE closet. She wheeled the hoop onto the blacktop and put it in the middle of our circle. It was different from regular basketball hoops 'cause it was all plastic except for the net, and it only stood about four feet high. It was made special for kids like Mrs. Aronson's.

We started out doing the stretches in the circle like the day before. Then we did some clapping exercises for coordination. After that, it was time to play basketball. Mrs. Aronson played some music on the boom box while we passed the ball around the circle. Every once in a while she'd stop the song, and whoever had the ball in their hands got to shoot for a basket. My job was to wheel the hoop around the circle in front of each player and go get the ball when they missed. A couple of them didn't really understand the rules of the game, and I had to coach them on when to pass or shoot. I could tell by the kids' faces that they were having the time of their lives playing hoops. They would clap excitedly even if they missed a shot. Just getting to touch the ball was making them happy. And seeing them get that happy made me happy.

As we played, I realized I missed Dontae. I was sure that

he would have had fun playing too. And once again when the bell rang, I didn't want to leave. It felt strange, but it seemed like the only time in my life I felt like I belonged was in Mrs. Aronson's class.

Walking home from school that day, I felt light again, like I had the day before.

"What's wrong with you?" Jesse asked.

It was just Jesse walking with me, so I felt safe enough to be honest.

"They got happy just touching the ball. And when they tried to make a basket, they missed most of the time, but they were still happy."

"What? The retards?"

"Man, don't say that."

"Sorry. Mrs. Aronson's class?"

"Yeah."

Jesse thought for second or two, and then said, "Yeah, it would suck to see other kids playing all the time and not be able to. And I guess when you get a chance to do the stuff regular kids do, you appreciate it more."

"That's what it is, man. They appreciate it more."

"Sounds like you like working in that class?"

"It's all right. It's pretty cool. Don't tell anybody I said that though."

"I won't."

Jesse wouldn't say anything, and that's why I told him the truth. If it had been Eduardo or Desi, I would have thought twice, but Jesse was cool.

When I got home that night, I put off reading *Islands in the Stream*. I was already past the halfway point in the book, and I kind of wanted Dontae to catch up with me so I wouldn't be too far ahead of him. I tried to do my work from Mrs. McHalenn's class. I knew she'd be all over me the next morning because I jetted, so I didn't want to go in empty-handed. Back at elementary school, I wouldn't care if a teacher tripped out over me not having my work done. But I didn't want Mrs. McHalenn pulling me out of social studies or Mrs. Aronson's class to finish my reading work, so I decided just to do it.

The next day I was eager to see if Dontae had made it to school. As I was going to my morning classes I kept glancing across the quad to the portable classrooms to see if I could catch a glimpse of him, but he wasn't there. And then when I got to English, Mrs. McHalenn was gunning for me. As soon as I walked through the door, she let me have it.

"Javier! Don't you ever pull that on me again! You will receive a two-week detention, plus clean-up detention, if you ever decide to sneak out of my room again! Is that understood?"

"Yeah, but I had to go to the bathroom."

"I don't want to hear it."

To take a little bite out of her bark, I handed her my work from the day before.

"Sit down," she said.

"Yes, ma'am."

*Whew*, I thought as I sat down at my desk. It could have gone a lot worse. She could have had the detention slip all written up and waiting for me. I was glad it blew over. Now I was cool for Aronson's and O'Neil's classes. McHalenn's class wasn't a complete wash either, because from out of nowhere she gave us a journal assignment to do. There was no topic, so I wrote a story about a sick kid who was stuck in a hospital. Everyone wondered why he was so sad, and it was because he couldn't do anything or go anywhere. The only person who understood was another sick kid he shared a room with. They wouldn't talk to each other about it. They just knew what the other was thinking.

The rest of the period went by smoothly, and so did Mr. O'Neil's. Near the end of social studies, I started getting excited about going to Mrs. Aronson's next. Mr. O'Neil noticed me tapping my foot and cleared his throat. I got the hint.

When the bell rang, I was off like a flash. I must have made it to Mrs. Aronson's in less than a minute. I heard, "NO! GO AWAY!" while I was still outside. *He's here*, I thought.

But once I walked through the door, I was surprised at what was going on. As the rest of the students worked normally at their desks Mrs. Aronson and Mrs. Rogers were standing around Dontae, who kept flinging things onto the ground. Books and other stuff were all over the floor. He was having a fit.

"NO! GO AWAY!" he called out again, his cheeks all red.

"Let's not be impolite, Dontae," Mrs. Aronson said calmly.

"NO! GO AWAY!"

"Okay, we're going to relax and just breathe," Mrs. Aronson coached.

"NO! GO AWAY!"

Then Dontae noticed me near the doorway. Like he'd been waiting for me since we stopped two days before, he said, "Read!"

Mrs. Aronson and Mrs. Rogers turned toward the doorway. I nodded at them.

"Ahhh. Your tutor is here," Mrs. Aronson said. "Perhaps he can read to you, Dontae? Dontae is having a rough morning, Javier. He's a bit upset today."

"That's okay. I'll read," I replied, making my way over to Dontae's desk.

After helping clean up Dontae's things, I pulled out *Islands in the Stream,* and we picked up where we left off. As I started reading, his eyes closed, then his mouth fell open, and he began to rock back and forth like he'd done before. His face became more peaceful. I still wasn't sure if he was understanding the story or not, but he sure seemed interested.

I was right in thinking Dontae would've enjoyed shooting hoops because at PE he was totally into it. He didn't make one basket, but like the others, he smiled every time he touched the ball.

After PE, Mrs. Aronson had to pick up lunches for the class at the cafeteria, so we walked together while the aide took the class back inside. Most times I'd have been worried about looking like a teacher's pet, but it didn't seem that way with Mrs. Aronson. It was almost as if we worked on the same job together or something, like we were coworkers.

"You sure came in handy this morning," she said.

"Me?" I asked.

"Yes, you. Dontae was having a really rough day."

"Why?"

"Put yourself in his shoes. Just because he's in my class doesn't mean he doesn't feel. He's human, and some days it's hard to be human. But he likes you."

"Really?"

"Oh yeah. My students are very sensitive. They know who's there to help them. They know where your heart is."

"Huh."

"It takes a very special person to work with my students. You're doing all right. Hang in there."

That sure threw me for a loop. I'd never been told that in my whole life about anything 'cause I'd never been good at anything. I just kind of ignored her comment. But after school as I was walking home with the guys it started to sink in. Eduardo and Desi were back, so they walked home with Jesse and me this time. They were still all bruised and bandaged up from the fight. They were happy though, mostly because of the forty bucks they'd gotten from Roberto. And because it was Friday and we'd survived our first week of middle school, they all felt like celebrating. All three of them slipped into the bushes for a long old time. They burned so much herb, the smoke was wafting out into the street. When they came out, they seemed like aliens wobbling back and forth. They were completely high. Funny—I was too, just not on herb.

# CHAPTER 5

Weeks passed by, and I got to work with Dontae most days. A lot of times when I'd show up to Mrs. Aronson's class, I could tell he'd been waiting for me. Sometimes he'd sit in his wheelchair with his hand on his cheek and a faraway look in his eyes, and when I'd walk through the door, he'd liven up. Then he'd start saying, "Read!" over and over again until I'd sit down at his desk. His eyes would follow my hands as I pulled the book out of my backpack, and they would widen when he caught a glimpse of the cover. I wondered why he liked that book so much. Sure, I was enjoying it, but why was he? The only words I'd ever heard him say were *no*, *go away*, and *read*. But as soon as I started, reading his eyes would close, and he'd begin to rock, and that peaceful look would come across his face.

*Islands* was a cool book. Every time I read it, it would make me forget everything else. When I read about the islands, and the ocean, and fishing, which I'd never done, it felt like I was doing it, right there with the characters. The story was set in the Caribbean, and I always thought of how cool it would be to actually see it someday. The book also had a lot of cursing and drinking. Whenever a curse word would come up, I'd always skip over it so I didn't say it out loud in front of Mrs. Aronson or her class.

On the days that I didn't get to work with Dontae, I'd work with one of Mrs. Aronson's other students, usually Nena. She would always smile at me when I sat down at her desk. I guess I was getting pretty good at signing 'cause I could sign *hello* and ask her how she was and all kinds of other things. She was a really good student. Sometimes she'd concentrate so hard on something, like writing her name, that she'd hold her breath. Then when she'd finish, she'd exhale like she'd just finished the hardest thing in the world. Or she'd sigh when she'd make a mistake, which made me feel really sad for her. If she got too down on herself, I would sign for her to take it easy, that she was doing really good.

Time was going by so fast, and before I knew it, it was Halloween week. Mrs. Aronson had all kinds of cool things planned for that Thursday. Because the students probably didn't get to go trick-or-treating, she was going to have them do it in class. They were going to wear costumes and have bags for candy and everything. They were even going to have a special lunch. All week the kids seemed kind of happy and anxious, like they were waiting for something to happen. It was fun, even for me. All the lessons I helped Dontae with had a Halloween theme and could be used as decorations for the classroom at the same time. By Wednesday the classroom was covered with all kinds of cutouts and drawings. There were black cats, vampires, witches, and ghosts everywhere. The students loved it.

Dontae was going to be a vampire. Mrs. Aronson had made him a cape from a black garbage bag, with a collar and everything. It looked really cool. I'd even found some plastic vampire fangs and fake blood at the convenience store by the school, so I swiped Dontae and myself both a set. Mrs. Aronson wanted us all to wear a costume for Halloween day, even the aide. I wasn't going to wear my stuff around school or anything. I'd just put mine on right before my work period and wear it for Mrs. Aronson's class. The excitement was even rubbing off on me, I guess. I kind of couldn't wait for the next day.

So things were going pretty good. But that all changed during PE. Eduardo was there, and it was good to see him 'cause he was usually on suspension or in the principal's office or something. We were playing football, and he was so excited to tell me something that he got benched for not paying attention to the plays. When he finally did tell me what was going on, I wished I'd never heard it. The big news was that Eduardo, Desi, Jesse, and I had all gotten invited to a high-school party because Roberto's girlfriend's brother was throwing it. There was going to be music, and beer, and girls and stuff. A lot of the Southside Playaz were going to be there. It was going to be hot, but I really didn't want to go. Of course, I didn't come right out and say that to Eduardo. I would've come off like the Punk of the Year. But with that many Playaz there, and booze and stuff, I just knew something was going to go down. My dad used to go to parties like that, and they always ended up bad. Fights would break out; somebody would have a gun. The cops would show up. I just didn't feel like being there for it. For a second I almost wished we were going trick-or-treating like we used to do. But I just nodded my head and said, "Cool, man."

The next day at school, everybody was psyched for Halloween. Some teachers and kids wore costumes. There were decorations up everywhere. The goth kids got extreme and showed up with all their gear on. They wore all kinds of rings with spiders and snakes on them, black nail polish, the works.

Even Mrs. McHalenn got dressed up. She wore a pirate dress and handed out popcorn balls to all of us. And in English she read "The Raven" by Edgar Allan Poe. She read it all spooky and acted it out really well. Then we saw a movie on Poe and had to do a work sheet about him.

Mr. O'Neil's class was special too. We got to watch a cartoon on the story of Ichabod Crane and the Headless Horseman. During the movie Mr. O'Neil passed out bowls of granola. One kid yelled out that it was hippie food, and Mr. O'Neil started to laugh. Before he let us go for the day, he asked us if we had any questions. I had one. It wasn't on the material, but for some dumb reason my hand shot up into the air. I'd been confused about something since the first day. When he called on me, I pointed to the posters of the rock stars on his wall, the ones that had the sign DON'T LET THIS HAPPEN TO YOU scrawled across them. Because they had been rich and famous, I asked him what that meant.

"Ah-ha, an inquiring mind would like to know something," Mr. O'Neil replied. "Simply put, it means don't squander your potential."

"Oh," I said, still a little confused but feeling like I shouldn't have asked in the first place.

By the time I got to Mrs. Aronson's, my day was going all right. As soon as I opened the door to her room, it was like the excitement whooshed out to greet me. The smells of lasagna and cake were in the air. The whole class was livelier than usual, laughing and clapping. Mrs. Aronson was wearing a witch costume and face paint and everything. She had on long green fingers with long nails too. The kids couldn't take their eyes off of her. She walked around the room checking their work and leaving little treats on their desks if they were doing well. Dontae was really having a good time too. I could tell he liked his costume. He was sitting much prouder in his wheelchair and kept turning his head to look at his cape.

The others in the class were all dressed up too. Nena had on a Cleopatra costume that Mrs. Aronson had made. She even wore an Egyptian-looking tiara that had little toy snakes on it. Lanzo dressed like a pirate with a patch over one eye. The aide had on a sweatshirt that made her look like a skeleton, and she carried a matching mask.

"Read!" Dontae said as soon as he saw me.

I sat down at his table and started to put my costume on. I didn't have a cape like his, but I'd worn my black jacket that day, so I flipped up the collar. Then I popped my fake Dracula teeth in and showed Dontae. His eyes widened as he reached out to touch them. I started laughing 'cause I didn't think he could figure out what happened to my real teeth; then I gave him the set I'd swiped for him. He held the plastic teeth in his hand and just looked at them for a while. He didn't understand what to do with them until Mrs. Aronson came by to help.

"Dontae!" she said excitedly. "You have more accessories! Let's put them in."

Carefully Mrs. Aronson slid on the fake teeth. Then she took the tube of fake blood, put some streaks on Dontae's face, and brought over a mirror. Dontae's eyes got really big when he saw himself, as if he couldn't believe that the face staring back was actually him. I couldn't feel all that guilty about swiping the teeth and blood at the convenience store after seeing how much Dontae enjoyed them.

"Read!" Dontae mumbled through his fake teeth, so I took out the *Islands* book and read with the fake teeth in my mouth.

I read for about ten minutes before Mrs. Aronson called

out that the trick or treating was about to start. A couple of the kids started clapping. I put the book away and got up to help out. As the aide and Mrs. Aronson ran around the room turning on spooky lights, all the students who could understand what was happening were smiling.

So no one would have to get up, Mrs. Aronson, the aide, and I went from table to table carrying bags full of treats. We had some candy, learning toys, raisins, popcorn balls, and toothbrushes, of all things. Our goal was to get the students to knock on their desks, and then we'd say, "Who is it?" And then they would to try to say trick or treat. I'd never seen happier faces in my life. As I went from table to table the faces got brighter and brighter, and there was nothing fake about them. Most of the kids couldn't say trick or treat. A couple could only kind of mumble the words. The only person who could say it clearly was Nena, and that was in sign language.

After trick or treating I got to stay for lunch. Mrs. Aronson kept calling me their special lunch guest. Because a lot of the class activities were life skills and socialization, they ate lunch in the classroom and did all the kitchen duties themselves. All her students had special jobs to do for lunch. They ran like clockwork. From putting the food on plates, to putting plates on the table, to setting out the utensils, even to cleaning up, they did it all. That's the one thing I kept learning in Mrs. Aronson's class, that the little things most people don't even think about might just be hardest things in the world to do for some people.

After lunch Mrs. Aronson called me over to her desk.

"Thanks for being our guest and helping out with the trick or treating, Javier."

Then of all things, she pulled her purse out of her desk and pulled out a five-dollar bill.

"Javier, I want to thank you for thinking of Dontae. Now I'm giving you five dollars for the teeth and the fake blood. I would like you to take it to whomever you owe the money to and pay them."

I was speechless. It was as if Mrs. Aronson could see right through me. How could she know that I'd swiped the stuff for Dontae? Then I remembered that first day at the library when she'd seen the book pop from under my shirt. She knew I was a thief, from my head right down to my hot shoes.

"And one last thing, Javier. If you need a book, just check it out in the library. That's what it's there for. And if you can't find one you like, ask somebody."

Then she opened up the cabinets behind her desk to show me that they were stacked full of books. Steinbeck. Zindel. London. She had them all.

"I was an English major in college," she explained. "I have cabinets full of books, so don't steal. It's a dangerous habit to have."

When I left Mrs. Aronson's that day, I thought about what Jesse had said about Jonah. *Damn*, I thought, *I get caught even when I don't get caught.*

Although I left feeling bad, lunch had been great. Halloween in general was turning out to be a very cool day. But as soon as I headed off to math, I remembered that the party was still on and the guys were expecting me to go. I hadn't figured out a way to get out of it. My mom was working late, and since she was trying to kick speed, she was going to church to meet with her prayer group after work, so she wouldn't even know if I'd gone or not. She was thinking that me and the guys were just going out to trick-or-treat like we'd always done. She figured I'd be home by eight and in bed by ten. The truth was that the party wasn't even going to start until about eight.

The guys were all psyched to go, even Jesse. His parents figured the same thing that my mom did, that we were just going trick-or-treating, so they didn't have a problem with letting him out. He'd been talking all week about how high he was going to get at the party. He went on about it so much that it made me wonder—I mean, he got really high all the time anyway, so what was the big deal? Eduardo and Desi were all excited because there were going to be girls there. I guess they'd been plotting on how to get themselves a couple of older girlfriends like Roberto's. His girlfriend, Ruby, was eighteen. She went to continuation school because she had a kid at sixteen. Her baby's daddy was going to be locked up in the pen for a very long time, so she hooked up with Roberto. To him it was nothing to have a girlfriend who was three years older and had a kid already. He wasn't just one of the Playaz, he was a real player.

Ruby had her own place. It wasn't much of a place, but it was hers. There were some real tiny apartments on Canyon Avenue, and Ruby was able to get into one. And from that point on, it became Roberto and Ruby's pad. When he wasn't in juvie or at a group home or something, he lived with Ruby. A lot of the Playaz would hide out there when the heat was on. Eduardo and Desi would even crash there some days when they were ditching school. They'd sit and game and eat chips all day.

Flaco was Ruby's brother. And since their parents were going to be in Mexico for a few days, Flaco was throwing the Halloween party at their house. The Playaz from our side of town were all invited, plus kids from the continuation school they went to. Flaco was a big-time tweaker. He was only seventeen and he'd already done two drug programs. But just as soon as he finished up his treatment, he'd go back on the tweak again. He'd do so much of it that he'd get rail thin, so that's where he got the name Flaco from. Whenever the guys would stop to talk to him about anything, I always got uncomfortable. He was so jumpy and jerky all the time from the meth that he made me jumpy and jerky too. Rumor had it he'd even break into people's houses and steal their stuff. If ever I was around him, I always felt like the cops were going to pop out from nowhere and we'd all get busted.

So that's the scene we were headed to that night. Even my dad, with all he'd done, would probably smack me upside the head if he knew I was going to a party like that. Even though he'd gotten busted for doing really hard-core stuff, he didn't want me to be mixed up in any of it. "Do what I say, and not what I do!" he'd tell me.

But that was just too hard sometimes. Eduardo, Desi, and Jesse were my friends. I had to go because that's what friends do. Saying no would have meant saying no to our friendship, then I'd be lost. Like it or not, I was down.

When I got home from school that afternoon, my mom was still at the apartment. She was getting ready for work and running around putting dinner out. I told her not to worry about it, that I'd make something for myself.

"I'm meeting my prayer group after work," she said as she laid out a plate for me.

"I know. I remember."

Right then I wanted to tell her that I was proud of her. That she was doing good with staying off the speed. But a part of me kept feeling like she might get more stressed if I said anything about it. I kept my mouth shut.

"All right, babe. I got to go. Lock the door," she said, grabbing her purse and keys. After the door closed behind her, I listened to her footsteps trot down the stairs, sad to see her go.

# CHAPTER 6

By seven that night it was pitch-black outside. Our neighborhood was full of little kids trick-or-treating, and the sounds of parties were coming in from all directions. For Flaco's party I shaved my head real close using my pop's clippers, then I put on a brand-new white T-shirt. I used some of my pop's aftershave so I'd smell good too. Eduardo said there'd be all kinds of girls at the party, so I didn't want to stink. After checking myself one last time, I slipped out of the apartment to wait on the curb. Eduardo and Jesse were going to meet me at my place, and then we'd walk over to Desi's and head to the party from there.

The streets were busy that night. Cars whizzed by bumping their stereos. Sometimes a carload of kids would speed past with girls shrieking and laughing out the windows. As I sat on the curb it hit me that maybe I could just go to be seen and then slip out when nobody was paying attention. Maybe they wouldn't even notice if I left.

Before they even got to my apartment, I could hear the guys clowning and laughing from down the street. They were both in a good mood. I forced a smile on my face when they reached me.

"You ready to roll, Javier?" Eduardo cried out upon seeing me.

"Let's do it!" I said back, getting up off the curb.

Eduardo and Jesse were all cleaned up too. They had on new white T-shirts and new baggie jeans. Jesse had on a new pair of Chuck T's too. We hadn't gone to the Farmers Market since the heist, so I guessed he must have paid for them fair and square. Desi was just as excited to go as the other guys. When we got to his house, he ran out to meet us on the sidewalk. We were all dressed alike. I wouldn't have blamed a cop for stopping us that night. We looked like a crew of gangbangers. On our way over to Flaco's parent's house, we passed kids and parents out trick-or-treating. Once again I wished that's what we were doing. But I guessed those days were over.

We could hear the party going on at Flaco's parents' house from a block away. The deep bass from the stereo was booming all over the neighborhood. You could smell a good barbecue coming from that direction too. If we hadn't known where the house was already, we could have found it by following the sounds and the smells. Then I started getting nervous 'cause I didn't know how I was supposed to act or what I was supposed to say. I wasn't funny like Eduardo, or crazy like Desi, or smart like Jesse. The best thing to do, I figured, was to not say or do anything. That way I wouldn't look stupid by acting dumb.

When we got to the house, there were tons of people inside and out in the backyard. The party was bumping already and it was only eight fifteen. There was a bouncer by the back gate, a huge three-hundred-pound homeboy. I didn't know his name, but I'd seen him around the neighborhood with some of the older Playaz. He looked about twenty-two. He had a shaved head and tattoos all up and down his arms. He waved us over by the back gate and quickly pulled out a wad of bills from his pants pocket. Just from the look, it might have been two hundred bucks right there in his hand. He then looked at us like he was waiting to get paid. I slid my hands into my pockets, but I knew that there wasn't anything in there. The five bucks Mrs. Aronson had given me for Dontae's Halloween stuff was already gone. I'd left it on the counter of the convenience store on my way home from school that afternoon. I hadn't even thought that there'd be a cover charge. And even if I had, I still didn't have any money. Coming to our rescue, Eduardo spoke up.

"Yo, check it out, man. Roberto invited us."

"Oh, Roberto. Oh, you're Eduardo, right?"

And he let us through, just like that. Roberto must have had some say 'cause the bouncer stepped aside like we were VIPs or something. From there we walked around the side of the house. The closer we got to the backyard, the louder everything got. The music was bumping and some people were dancing, but most were talking in little groups. Flaco and some other homeboys were working the barbecue grill, doing up some carne asada. A lot of the kids had costumes on. There were girls everywhere. A few of the girls I even recognized from school. They were mostly eighth-graders, but they looked like high schoolers done up. And everybody was drinking beer.

"YO!" we heard from across the party as Roberto zigzagged through the crowd to greet us.

"Hey! Wassup, guys?"

By his glowing red face, I could tell he was trashed. He was smiling, which I'd never seen him do. Still, I tried not to stand too close to him. Roberto was like a wild wolf, like if you looked at him too hard, he might attack you or something.

"You need *cerveza*, homeboys," he said, and then led us from the backyard into the house.

In the kitchen there were kids standing around everywhere. Plastic garbage bags were covering the kitchen table, and on top were three big ice chests full of beer. There must have been about twenty cases dumped into the ice. Empty boxes were all over the kitchen floor and counters. Roberto dug around and pulled out cans for me and the guys. We opened them and started sipping. My first swallow of beer tasted like tar, but I played it cool.

"OHHH NOOO!" I heard from behind me. I knew that voice anywhere. Enrique.

"Check out this punk-ass bitch!" he wailed. "There ain't no retards at this party, so you better take your bitch ass home!"

The guys were watching. There was no way I could let it slide or play it off. The ball was in my court, so I had to play.

"Fuck you, punk!" I shouted to him.

Enrique lunged for me. Jumping through some kids, he got pretty close to me before some older homeboys hustled in between us. The older guys were cracking up as they kept us apart.

"Dammnn! These little homies don't play!" one of them cried.

"Shiitt, y'all need to chill out. This is a party!" Roberto said while laughing.

Eduardo and the guys spun me around and guided me into the front room of the house. The room was really nice with some sofas, a coffee table, and a big picture-frame window. A few couples were making out in there, and one girl was passed out drunk on the floor. There was some room on the couch facing the big window, so I fell into it. Jesse sat next to me and started packing his pipe with herb.

"How'd I do?" I asked him.

78

Jesse smiled. "You played it pretty cool. I knew you were scared as hell, but he didn't."

I smiled and tried to sip some beer, but the taste wasn't getting any better. Kicking back, I watched the people for a while. The girls were all pretty. A couple of high-school girls came and sat down on the other side of the sofa. One was dressed like a fairy princess with a magic wand and everything, and the other one had on the wicked nurse outfit from *Kill Bill*. They talked nonstop about people they knew and things that had happened that day at school. I didn't say a word to them and just pretended I wasn't paying attention to what they were saying. Ruby came by a couple of times to ask us if were having a good time. While we were inside, Eduardo and Desi were out in the back trying to talk to more girls.

From out of the corner of my eye, I watched Jesse. He didn't care what was going on. He'd come to the party to get high, and that's what he was doing. He'd light his pipe, take a long drag on it, hold his breath for what seemed like a whole minute, then exhale. Cracking open a fresh beer, he'd drink down half the can before coming up for air. He'd do that a couple of times, then lean back for like ten minutes before doing it again. In hardly no time at all, he was wasted. But the music was still going, and everything seemed cool.

With the music, and so many people, and so much talking, I guess I must've zoned out or something. All of a sudden I was scared almost to death when some loud firecrackers blasted off in front of the house. Since we were facing the big window, I looked in that direction, but the curtains were closed, so I couldn't see out to the front yard or the street. Then I got confused 'cause it sounded like somebody was throwing coins on the wall behind me. I felt a breeze of cool air and looked up just as little puffs of dust were popping out of the wall. Then I heard glass breaking as the windows were shattering. *Shit!* I thought. *It's not firecrackers. It's gunshots. They're shooting!*

Girls started to scream, and things crashed to the floor. Jesse was so out of it, I had to grab him by the shoulders and throw him down. One of the high-school girls sitting on the couch with us started to panic. She stood straight up in the middle of the room, screaming and cursing. More cursing and shouting came from the backyard, and a second later tons of people started running into the house to find out what was happening. As I was about to stand up, a loud series of shots rang out again. POW-POW-POW-POW-POW-POW-POW! Tires squealed out front as a car sped off.

Scrambling through the people, Flaco ran into the front room still holding some barbecue tongs. He saw the girl screaming in the middle of the room, so he jumped her and brought her down to the floor. Everybody was going crazy and panicking.

"WHO WAS IT?"

"WHAT THE FUCK HAPPENED?"

I just stayed low to the floor, hanging on to Jesse. He was so stoned, he still didn't know what was going on. Next thing I knew, Roberto ran into the room with a serious look on his face. He was gripping something black and holding it cautiously away from people. A gun.

*Shit*, I thought. *Time to go.*

Roberto carefully walked up to the window, pulled the curtain aside, and peered out. Turning around, he scanned the room and noticed me. He came straight over to me and squatted down. Looking me dead in the eye with the most serious look I'd ever seen on his face, he asked, "What happened?" At that moment I knew why Roberto had so much clout with the Playaz. In the midst of a storm, he was ice-cold cool.

I was so scared, I didn't even think I could speak. I wanted to cry, and I could feel the little pins and needles in the corners of my eyes that meant it was coming. For a split second I thought about how big a punk I'd look like if I just fell apart right there in front of everybody. But then, like a ventriloquist was controlling my mouth, "drive-by" fell out.

"Drive-by?" Roberto clarified.

I nodded and said it again, "Drive-by." Looking up over Roberto's shoulders, I saw four or five older homeboys standing around waiting for the order. Roberto got up to talk to them. Two or three were clutching guns too. *This is messed up*, I thought. I had to get out of there. Cutting through the people, Eduardo and Desi ran over to where I was. They asked me the same question that Roberto had. "Drive-by" fell out of my mouth again. Flaco got up off the floor and started yelling out, "Is everybody okay? Did anybody get hit?" Then he started cursing up a storm. He was way tweaked out, with his jaw twitching and everything. He paced around, still cursing and still holding those barbecue tongs. It was a crazy scene. It couldn't have gotten any worse. But then I overheard Roberto and the guys say, "Let's jet!"

From what I was getting from the Playazes' conversation, they knew the Northsiders had shot up the party. So they wanted to cruise up there to find a group of them and do some payback.

"We roll, then!" one of them said.

"Let's roll!" Roberto repeated.

By then, Eduardo and Desi were standing with the older Playaz. They stayed quiet, but I noticed a sparkle in their eyes, like they wanted to be in on it. Of all things, I suddenly thought about looking into the eyes of Mrs. Aronson's kids earlier that day while they were trick-or-treating, and how happy they were. How could a day go from that to this? As I sat there on the floor with Jesse sprawled out stoned, I hoped we were inconspicuous. Momentum was building for the payback run as the guys were grabbing their coats and keys. I didn't want to roll with them.

Even though there were some older homeboys there, Roberto took charge. He said who was riding with whom. He told them where they were going. He laid out the plan. Nearby, Ruby was a mess. She stood with her arms crossed, pleading with him not to go. A few tears fell from her eyes, but Roberto ignored her. For a second I wondered where her baby was.

Gradually the gang of Playaz made their way to the front yard. I stayed put and listened to them outside. Most of the party followed them and looked on as they got into their cars to go. They hadn't even asked me to roll with them, but Eduardo and Desi were going, and they were psyched. I waited until I heard them close their car doors, start their engines, and pull off. People were coming back into the house to gather up their stuff to leave. Jesse was still stoned. I thought about just leaving him there and going home, but I couldn't do it.

"Jesse," I said as I shook him.

"What, man?" he replied groggily.

"Let's go."

"Did the shooting stop?"

"Yeah, it stopped, man. Let's go."

Heavy as he was, I dragged him up off the floor. He could walk a little, but I had to guide him out of the house.

"You drank too much, man!" I said to him as I struggled to keep him on the sidewalk.

"I know. I'm messed up."

"You need to snap out of it. I have to go home."

"All right."

I couldn't take Jesse home like that. His parents would have freaked out on him. It was ten fifteen already and my mom would be home by about eleven, so I only had maybe a half hour to sober him up. With my arm over his shoulder, I walked him to the gas station on the corner of Canyon Avenue. I leaned him against the wall by the bathroom and ran to get the key from the attendant. When I got back, Jesse had slipped down the wall and was on his knees. I finally got him into the bathroom and balanced him against the sink. Then I turned on the cold water and shoved his head under it.

"Wha-you-doing?" he gurgled.

"I read it in a book. Maybe it'll work."

"Oh."

Jesse stayed under the faucet for a good ten minutes. When he finally lifted his head up, he seemed more himself. I gave him some paper towels to dry off with, and we left. It was getting late, so we hustled back to our neighborhood. Jesse had to puke twice on the way, but he was in much better shape than he was at the party. Every now and then we'd hear sirens in the distance. He and I didn't look at each other, but I figured we both knew we were thinking the same thing.

"You thinking that too?" Jesse asked me.

"That the sirens could be for them? That they might be dead or something?"

"Yeah."

"Well, yeah."

"Shit, they're all right. This ain't LA. This is Orbe Nuevo! Just a bunch of wannabe gangsters. This ain't no real hood!"

I laughed when Jesse put it like that, but I knew he was worried too. Both his brothers were locked up for gangbanging. One of them was doing hard time for attempted murder. Jesse knew it could get hard-core right here in our hood. He was trying to make us feel better, just whistling past the graveyard.

I got home at ten to eleven, right on time. I hurried to make myself a sandwich and get out of my clothes, then I switched off the light and jumped into bed. Minutes passed as I waited for my mom to get home. Eventually I heard the familiar sounds of her footsteps on the stairs and her keys jingling as she unlocked the front door. I closed my eyes as I heard her stop in front of my doorway before walking into the kitchen. I listened as she opened the mail, made herself something to eat, and then finally crashed out on the couch in front of the TV. If she only knew what had gone on that night. In the distance I could still hear sirens wailing across the city. Again and again I kept thinking the same thing. Eduardo and Desi were out there in it. Those sirens might be for them. They might be dead.

# CHAPTER 7

Somewhere between Halloween night and the next morning, I'd had enough. I didn't want my life to be like this. Over and over again I kept thinking about the guys. Did they do something up on the northside? Were they all right? The scene had been so crazy at Flaco's that it hadn't really sunk in until I was trying to sleep. I turned and rolled all night, thinking about the drive-by and all that screaming and cursing. I might have slept thirty minutes, total. By morning the last place I wanted to go was school. If I could just make it to Mrs. Aronson's, I told myself, I'd be all right.

At school I felt like a zombie walking around for the first few periods. I didn't even feel close to being myself until Mr. O'Neil's class. There was still no sign of Eduardo or Desi. All morning long I heard people talking about what went down at Flaco and Ruby's party, but they had it all wrong. Some kids were saying some Northsiders crashed the party and there was a big fight. Other kids said a couple of people got shot. I wasn't about to rat, so I didn't set them straight. Only a few of us from Orbe Nuevo had actually been there, and I didn't see any of them at school. Maybe they'd all stayed home. Maybe I was the only dweeb who'd gone to school that day.

And then, to top everything off, Mr. O'Neil threw some

huge term project at us. Working with a partner, we were supposed to take a poem or a song from an assigned century and put it into historical context.

"Now, I chose each poem based on what I've gathered to be your personal interests," he said as he handed out our poems. "Your century and partner's name is in the upper right-hand corner of your poem sheet, so you can jump right into the project. Start out with a simple KWL chart and see what you can come up with by the end of class. Use your textbooks or any other periodicals you can find in the room. Let's go! Let's get on it!"

My poem was from the twentieth century. It was titled "End of the Night" and was written by a guy named Jim Morrison. I'd never heard of the poem or the writer before. Then all of sudden a goth girl named Jessica walked up to my desk.

"Are you Javier–Twentieth Century?" she mumbled.

"Yeah," I replied.

"Then you're my partner."

"Oh," I said, then tried to clear some space on my desk so we could work.

She grabbed an empty desk and spun it around so she could face me, and then she sat down.

"I'm Jessica."

"Javier."

"Who'd you get?"

"I got 'End of the Night' by Jim Morrison. You?"

"Jim Morrison, cool!" she nodded. "I got 'Hazy Shade of Winter' by Simon and Garfunkel."

"Who?"

"Simon and Garfunkel. They're famous."

"Oh," I replied, wondering where.

She was smart. Smart and white. She was a goth girl with jet-black hair, but her eyebrows were blond. She wore clunky black-framed glasses, and her hair was everywhere. She was wearing all black with black nail polish. It looked like she'd even had on some dark black-red lipstick earlier, but it was wearing off. I watched as she pulled out two blank pieces of paper and started to make the KWL charts. Her writing was neat, but she was a lefty and it seemed like she was stabbing the paper every time she wrote. She had on about six rings covered with skulls and snakes.

I'd seen Jessica around the school before, but she was new to Orbe Nuevo. She always got picked up after school in a big Hummer. Her dad was some kind of military pilot or something, so she'd lived all over the world. She even spoke a few languages. Because she was white, some of the Mexican girls gave her the cold shoulder. Even though it was mean and all, and it wasn't very cool, that's the way it was. Jessica's best friend was a black girl named Latrice, who was goth too. But even though they were both goth girls, they were outcasts as far as the Mexican goth girls were concerned.

Jessica was really, really smart too, like Jesse-smart, but maybe even smarter. She should have been in high achievers except that she didn't care about grades or homework or stuff like that. I had math and science with her too, and sometimes Mr. Abbott, our teacher, would be kind of worn-out from the day, so he'd make some mistakes or misspeak. Jessica would always be there to catch him. The rest of us would be all, "Huh? What's she talking about?" But she'd be right. And Mr. Abbott would apologize, then thank her for correcting him.

"So what do you know about Jim Morrison?" Jessica asked me, with her pen hovering over the paper.

"Nothing."

"Jim Morrison? Jim Morrison and the Doors? You've never heard of him?"

"No," I said defensively.

"Well, other than being that guy on the wall over there," she said as she pointed to one of Mr. O'Neil's posters of a white guy with long hair, "he's, like, really famous. The Doors had a ton of hits and were on the top of the charts in the sixties. Just like mine, Simon and Garfunkel. They were really big then too."

"Oh. So put that down, girl!"

Jessica smiled.

"You're crazy, Javier–Twentieth Century," Jessica said as she started to fill out the chart. "So what else do you want to know?"

"How come you smell like cigarettes?"

Panicking all of sudden, she whispered, "Shut up!" then turned to see if Mr. O'Neil was around.

I had to laugh. She seemed so scared that Mr. O'Neil would find out she smoked.

"So what do you want to know about Jim Morrison?"

"Ohhh," I sang, trying to play dumb. "Um, well, what he was about, I guess."

Jessica wrote that down.

"Oh! I have an idea. We can get some pictures of hippies and Vietnam and stuff and make a little video for our project."

"How?"

"It's easy. We can just do it on a laptop!"

"Laptop? Rich girl!" I sighed.

"I'm not rich."

"How come you got a Hummer, then?"

"Because my dad spends more than he can afford. My dad's in the military. They don't make a lot."

"Oh."

Jessica and I worked on our project for the rest of class. She seemed pretty cool, and I was glad that she was my partner. I learned that she was an only child like me, and that she actually lived on the northside of town, but the schools up there had been full by the time she'd signed up in our district. That's why she was going to Orbe Nuevo. She said she liked it better anyway, even though she didn't have a lot of friends. Her pop was a helicopter pilot and he'd been in the wars in Iraq and Afghanistan, and her mom was a drunk her dad had left down South. Jessica was born in a military hospital in Germany, and she could speak German, and French, and some Chamorro and Tagalog 'cause she lived in Guam for a while. And she knew Spanish a lot better than me, but she made me promise not to tell anybody. When I asked her why, she explained that she liked to know when people were talking trash about her without them knowing that she knew.

The poem Mr. O'Neil gave me was way intense. It was really simple, but it was really complicated too. As I read the words I couldn't help thinking that Mr. O'Neil must've known I'd spent the night before tossing and turning. I got the feeling that Jim Morrison must have been talking about Orbe Nuevo when he wrote "End of the Night." With the highway, the night, and everything, it seemed like it was a poem about my life. When the bell rang, I shoved the poem into my backpack. Jessica whipped out her cell phone and started thumbing in digits.

"Give me your cell number so if I find some stuff for the video, I can call you."

I just looked at her blankly.

Puzzled by my look, she asked, "What?"

"Not everybody has a cell phone."

"Oh. Email?"

I gave her the same look.

"You don't have email? All right, land line?"

I gave her my phone number.

"Javier–Twentieth Century," she said as she thumbed that in for my name.

*Finally*, I thought, as I made it to the door of Mrs. Aronson's class. It was the only place I wanted to be right then, and as soon as I walked in, I felt better. Dontae was there finishing up some of his morning work. He could handle a pencil a lot better than Lanzo, but his letters were all misshapen and unaligned. His assignment was to copy down his address and phone number three times, but he could barely do it once. When he was able to make a letter that looked mostly like it was supposed to, I gave him a thumbs-up and fist pump. He'd just look at me like he wasn't sure what I meant.

By the time I got to read to him, I'd stopped thinking about what had happened the night before. I wasn't worried about the guys or the drive-by or anything. Actually, the more I worked with the kids in Mrs. Aronson's class, the more I got this weird feeling that *I* was the one in special ed and that Dontae and the other kids were my teachers. Even though most of them could barely speak or write or do most things other kids could do, they were taking me out of myself.

Lunch came, and Jesse wasn't in the cafeteria to eat with me. I felt like an alien. I grabbed my lunch off the tray and went outside to eat up against the wall where a lot of kids who didn't have anybody to eat with would go. There I was, one of them. Looking down the wall, I saw Jessica and Latrice doing the same thing, except they were laughing and clowning with each other. I probably could have just gone and sat down with them, but that would have made me look too desperate. If Eduardo had liked one of them, he could have pulled it off, but not me. I didn't have his guts or his goofy cool.

After eating, I pulled out *Islands* and pretended to read for a while. It didn't feel right to read it without Dontae, like I was going behind his back or something. Instead of reading the story, I glossed over the foreword about Hemingway, and man was that guy a trip. He'd been all over the world, and he'd done everything. So that's why everything seemed so real in the story.

I made it through the rest of the day and was glad to see Jesse waiting for me on the sidewalk after school. As I was walking over to him a big Hummer pulled up. Jessica ran past me and climbed in.

"Later, Javier–Twentieth Century!" she called out to me.

I nodded and made my way over to Jesse.

"What's up?" he called out.

"What's up, man?"

We started walking home and he told me why he hadn't been at school that day.

"I was *hungover*, man!"

I started laughing.

"Yeah, you were pretty trashed," I replied.

"But that's not the news."

I readied myself for the worst news possible because I'd imagined it all night long. Eduardo and Desi had been hit in a shootout with some Northsiders. Or they got wrecked in Roberto's car. Something terrible like that had happened, I just knew it.

"You ready?" Jesse asked me.

"Go, man! Tell me what happened."

"So I'm like sick and puking all night long, right? I didn't get much sleep. So at about two in the morning I hear this screaming and yelling coming from next door. I look out my window and the lights are on in Eduardo's house. I could hear his mom crying. So my mom wakes up and goes over next door to find out what happened."

"Yeah?" I asked.

"When my mom gets back, I hear her down the hall telling the story to my dad."

"And?"

"Roberto, Eduardo, Flaco, and Desi all got popped by the cops last night. They'd been rolling around the Northside for like ten minutes when some county sheriffs pulled them over. They sat them down on the sidewalk. And then they bring in the drug-sniffing dog. The dog finds Roberto's gun under the seat of the car."

"No way!"

"So they get nailed. They're all at juvie right now. Flaco and Roberto are getting sent back to YA."

"No way!"

"They wrote them up for everything. Gang association, underage driving, driving without a license, driving a stolen vehicle, possession of a concealed weapon, underage drinking. Flaco was so spun out, he didn't even know he had some meth in his wallet. In his wallet, man! The stuff fell right out when the cops were checking his ID."

"Shit!"

"We dodged a bullet last night, man!"

"No shit!"

"We could have been in that car!"

"I know."

Jesse was right. If I hadn't been so scared, and if Jesse hadn't been so faded, we probably would have been right there with them when it all went down. In a weird way, my being an oddball—and Jesse being high—actually helped.

A part of me felt kind of relieved that the guys were going to be locked up. This way, I wouldn't have to worry about them like I did the night before. On the other hand, it was me that I was worried about now. I didn't have a lot of friends as it was, and now that two more would be out for a while, well, middle school just seemed scary. If Jesse wasn't there, I'd be all alone. Sure I had Mrs. Aronson's class, but I couldn't live there.

"Thanks, man," Jesse said from out of nowhere.

"For what?"

"For helping me out last night."

"I couldn't just leave you there."

"I would have," he said with a chuckle. "So what's with that goth-gringa?"

I didn't think he'd noticed when Jessica had said bye to me.

"Just a friend."

"She rich?"

"I don't know. She says she isn't, but they got a Hummer."

"A lot of rich people say they aren't rich," Jesse said knowingly.

"Really? Why?"

"So people won't ask them to share!" he said with a grin.

We laughed pretty much the whole way home. I think Jesse

was relieved too that the guys got busted and put on ice. He worried about them just as much as I did, maybe even more. Every now and then I'd think that maybe the reason why he smoked so much herb was because he was too sensitive to things. For him, getting high was a break from feeling too much all the time.

After Jesse and I went our separate ways, my surprise of the afternoon came when I turned the corner and saw a man sitting on the steps of our apartment building. He wore jeans, a plaid flannel shirt, and a pair of bright white sneakers. Beside him lay a clear plastic garbage bag stuffed with clothes, files, a few books, and a leather jacket. He had a mustache and was smoking a cigarette, watching me walk down the sidewalk. As I got closer to him I realized who it was.

"Hey, *mijo!*" my pop called out.

I wanted to run up and hug him, but I knew that wouldn't look cool, so I just casually strolled over. He took a drag off his cigarette and carefully put it on the step, then stood up to give me a hug. Laughing, he explained that he'd been home for hours but didn't have his key to the apartment. As we were hugging and shaking hands I felt on top of the world. Pop was actually home! But for how long?

# CHAPTER 8

Having my pop home meant a lot of things. It meant that there was somebody in the apartment every day when I got back from school and that somebody could also answer the phone if I got into trouble. When I got home, he would bug me about my homework, and he'd even check it sometimes, which my mom wouldn't do. He'd always make everything a life lesson too, saying things like, "Don't screw up in school or you're going to pay for it for a long time," or, "Don't run around with those wannabe *cholos* or you'll end up picking up a case!" But most of the time, if I wasn't getting into trouble, it was pretty cool having him around.

My pop had a 1967 Plymouth that had belonged to his pop. He kept it over at my *abuela*'s when he was locked up. When he was out, he'd have a friend tow the car over to the apartment and he'd work on it when he wasn't looking for a job. It was primer gray, and the seats were dusty and ragged. It sounded really powerful and smoked a lot when it ran. When I got home from school in the afternoons, the hood would be open and my pop would be somewhere under it. I'd throw my backpack in the apartment, then run out to help him.

When the Plymouth was running, every few days or so, we'd take rides around town, mostly to the auto parts store or for a burger or whatever. That's the happiest I'd ever seen him, when he was driving his Plymouth. He'd gun it sometimes and lay patch at stops signs, or he'd cruise real slowly if he saw some women on the streets. He'd give them a long look, then stomp on the gas to peel off.

As we rode around he'd tell me stories about when he was a teenager and all the crazy things he'd done back then, like cruising the streets with his homeboys and filling the Plymouth's trunk up with beer and not coming home until all the beer was gone. His favorite story was one about how he'd partied all night long in one town and somehow woke up the next morning by the side of the road with no shirt or shoes—two counties away. He had to walk barefoot for miles before an eighteen-wheeler stopped and gave him a ride back to Orbe Nuevo. When he'd tell me that story, he'd get all excited and his eyes would light up like it was the first time telling it. He'd smile and laugh like crazy.

One afternoon we had burgers at a restaurant and talked.

"So, you got a girlfriend?" he asked.

"Nah."

"That's smart. Don't get mixed up in anything serious yet. You don't even know what you want to do for work. And then you don't even know if you can do it. That's two different things. You hear me?"

"Yeah."

"I mean, it's easy to say you want to do something, but can you see the path? Shoot, man. I wanted to do a lot of things, but I had no idea how to even start. And then sometimes you do see the path, but it gets blurry again. You hear me?"

"Yeah."

"So you thought about anything yet?"

The only thing I'd been thinking about lately was what Mrs. Aronson did. Maybe I could try to do that, or be a teacher's aide, even. But I didn't want to sound soft around my pop. So I lied and said something else.

"Mechanic or machinist, maybe," I replied.

"That's good. Those are good trades. But look around. See what people are looking for. Sometimes you can spot what they're going to need early and then get a skill for that."

I nodded because my pop's advice made sense.

My mom's first reaction to having my pop home was that she'd liven up some and get happier. She also felt relieved, I think, 'cause she wasn't the only one watching me. When she got home from work, I'd hear her chatting away, telling him about her day. Having pop home meant that she had somebody to listen to her. She stayed clean too because she was too busy being suspicious about him partying. But eventually they'd argue, usually about money.

My mom didn't earn much at her job, even with the over-time, so when my pop came home, just that extra person meant more money for food, electricity, and even water. My pop would usually come out of the joint with the few dollars he had on the books, but that would only last him a couple of weeks on the outside. After that, he'd start asking my mom for cash. Then she'd start to yell at him. "When are you going to get a job?" "Did you look for a job?" "How come you can't keep a job?" My pop would get fed up with hearing that all the time, so he'd go over to my abuela's for an hour or two. Those hour or twos would then stretch to overnight. Over in my abuela's neighborhood, my pop would run into his old friends. They'd sit up all night drinking. Then the drinking would become herb, and the herb would become speed.

After my pop had been home two weeks, it became a waiting game for me. I knew he was going to get busted; the only question was when. He'd been sleeping over at my abuela's house to avoid dealing with my mom. And then I wouldn't see him for a couple of days at a time. The times that I did see him, his face would be all red, his eyes would be bugging out, and he'd look stressed-out and panicked, like he knew he was screwing up but couldn't do anything about it. Then exactly two weeks and three days after he'd gotten out, the call came through. My mom was at work, so I answered the phone.

"Javier?" my pop said over the phone.

"Yeah?"

"It's me."

"What's up?"

"I'm down here at county lockup. Got popped for a parole violation."

"What happened?"

"I pissed a dirty test. They're going to send me back to the pen."

"Oh."

"Tell your mom I called. I'll call her in a few weeks."

"Okay."

"You take care of business, mijo."

"All right."

"Bye."

"Bye."

My pop caught me before I hung up.

"Hey, Javier?"

"Yeah?"

"Sorry. The path got blurry again."

And that was it. My pop was gone again, just like that.

# CHAPTER 9

Right about that time, Jesse and Desi got out of juvie. They'd
spent a week and a half in there while the courts sorted out
the whole mess with the stolen car and gun, and by the time
they got back to school, they had become legends. Word had
gotten out that they were in real deep with a gang and had
done something serious. Some kids said they'd beat down
some Northsiders. Other kids said they'd done a hit. The truth
hadn't really come out because everybody who'd actually
been to the party was on a no-rat notice, including Jesse and
me. We couldn't mention anything about Halloween night to
anybody, or we'd risk getting slammed by the older homeboys
in our set. It didn't bother me, 'cause I didn't want to talk about
it anyway.

But Eduardo and Desi were quick to lock on to any kind
of street cred they could get. They liked being feared. Even
eighth-graders made way for them when they walked around
school. All kinds of girls were talking to them, and every day
almost, it seemed like they were walking home with different ones. I learned a lot about what kids would do in middle school just to be seen with somebody they thought was
cool. Kids Eduardo and Desi hadn't even spoken to before

were offering to do their homework or loan them games or whatever.

Somehow, I guess because Roberto got sent back to YA and all, Eduardo and Desi picked up his job of helping out with business for the Playaz. They always had money now, and not just the dollar or two for lunch, but mad dinero, like having eighty to a hundred bucks on them all the time. They could buy whatever they wanted, and they'd treat whenever we hung out. They had real flashy clothes too, and chains and stuff. Eduardo must've had about five new pairs of sneakers, all old-school. Desi got them both cell phones. I thought it was cool and all, but I didn't go crazy like some of the other kids did.

Another thing was that they were speaking in a different language now that was all glances and signals. I couldn't decipher much of it, but I knew something was up when one of them would look at the other and just nod or something, and then the other would suddenly have to text or call somebody. Ruby had something to do with it all 'cause she'd show up after school pushing her baby around in a stroller, and when the guys caught a glimpse of her, they'd have to ride with her to take care of some business. Jesse and I never talked about it, but I knew he was wondering what was up, just like me.

Jesse was enjoying the perks of having two friends who were out hustling and making connections 'cause once the guys got back from juvie, herb was nothing for them to get their hands on, and for free. They never sold it to Jesse. It was all between friends, and now he had an unlimited supply. I mean it wasn't like Jesse'd had trouble getting it or anything before, but now it wasn't even an issue. He stayed high most of the time. I'll never forget that day we walked to school together and he got loaded on the way, and then during a special assembly in first period, he was called up front to accept an achievement award. Everybody clapped and howled for him. The teachers and principal were all smiling. And there he was, taking the award flat-out stoned. As I watched him I kind of wished that I were smart enough to be stoned all the time and still get As in school.

After my pop got locked up again, I went back to my old routine. When he'd been home, it was like I had something more to look forward to throughout the day. But now that he was gone, all I had was Mrs. Aronson's class again. I didn't mind though; I was just glad to have something. No matter what, Dontae and the other kids needed me, and that felt nice, I guess. Mrs. Aronson once told me that her students were very sensitive, that they could tell things about me that other people couldn't. I didn't believe her at the time, but then I showed up to class the day after my dad got locked up. I'd only been there long enough to put my backpack down and take my coat off when Lanzo, who didn't even like to get touched, got up, walked over to me, and gave me a hug. I wasn't letting anybody else know I was down, but Lanzo knew. He could sense it.

Then that very same day, Dontae wasn't himself either. Instead of closing his eyes and rocking like he usually did when I read to him, he just looked at me, like he was waiting for me to tell him why I was down. I could see in his eyes that he knew I wasn't myself.

At least the project Jessica and I were working on was turning out to be pretty interesting. Jessica kept bringing me Jim

Morrison articles and stuff from off the net. She had the songs of our poems on her phone, and sometimes during in-class project time we'd listen to them. I had to admit, "End of the Night" was pretty cool in a spooky kind of way. And her song, "Hazy Shade of Winter," really made you think about noticing the changes in time. Jessica even got into the habit of calling me at night to tell me when she found something cool for our project. I got the sense she was like me in a way, kind of short on friends. And when she got home from school, nobody was at her house either. Her pop had a second job at an airfield, so she'd get dropped off at home, and then she'd have to wait until eight or nine for her pop to get off from work. Though sometimes Latrice would be over at her house when she called, laughing and goofing in the background.

Jessica got really swept up into the project. It seemed to be the only schoolwork she would do. I asked her why one time in class, and she answered, "Because I like projects. I have OCD tendencies."

"What's that?" I asked her.

"Obsessive compulsive disorder. I get unusually preoccupied with details and completing tasks that have a viewable result."

"What?" I asked, even more confused.

"I like projects and do them well because I can get all into them, and you can see them when they're done, and you can see if you did them well or not."

"Oh."

"And I'm ADD, which means that ordinary tasks, like everyday homework, don't hold my attention for very long."

"Oh. So why aren't you special ed or something?"

"My dad wants me mainstreamed."

"Huh?"

"My dad wants me in regular classes."

"If you got all that stuff, then how come you're so smart?"

"You think I'm smart?" Jessica replied with light in her eyes and a smile I'd never seen on her face before.

"Kinda."

"Really?"

"Yeah."

I guessed Jessica had never been told she was smart, 'cause she acted totally surprised. Then she was looking at me funny, all intense like she liked me or something, so I changed the subject and started talking about our project again.

When I stepped into math class later that day, I felt my heart drop into my stomach. Jessica had changed desks so she now sat right next to me. She'd been clear across the room before. I didn't say anything to her, but just sat down at my desk. She was drawing on her notebook and didn't look up. If she liked me, she was really cool about it. She made it seem like it was the most natural thing in the world to be at the next desk over. I didn't want to trip out over it all, so I played it cool like her.

As I sat there I started thinking about Thanksgiving break coming up the next week and how I'd mostly be by myself. That was one thing I realized right then about school: at least you had other people around you all day, even if you didn't really know them or say anything to them. But a whole week at home with nothing but regular TV and ramen noodles was already making me lonely. Eduardo and Desi were spending a lot of time with Ruby lately. Ruby would drive the guys all over town to do stuff. There was static on the streets because of the Halloween night drive-by. The scene with the Playaz and the Northsiders was a steaming volcano ready to explode. And I knew that my friends were somehow, some way, going to be in the middle of it.

# CHAPTER 10

Thanksgiving break seemed to come faster this year. To be honest, I didn't want to take the break from school. Mrs. Aronson's class had become the best part of my day, like they were my real family while everything else in my life seemed phony. But there I was, stuck in the apartment all by myself. My mom worked doubles most days, so she'd be leaving out the door right about the time I was waking up.

"Don't watch too much TV. If you want to go somewhere, call me first. If you have an emergency, knock on Mrs. Durran's, next door!"

Sleepily, I'd nod and wave until she'd left. Then I'd take my bowl of cereal over to the couch to watch TV. It was exactly four hours from the time my mom left for work until Springer came on, which was the only show on daytime TV that was halfway cool. Before Springer, there was nothing on but news talk shows and baby cartoons. So after breakfast that first Monday morning of break, I broke out a new book and started reading until Springer. Mrs. Aronson lent me something like ten books for the week, and with nothing on TV, I thought I might run out by Wednesday.

Mrs. Aronson had left early on Thursday for her Thanksgiving break. She and her family were going to New York. She was from there and seemed real excited to go back home. On her last day she nervously rushed from one thing to the next to set up the class for the sub. And then as I was about to leave for lunch, she called me over to the cabinets behind her desk. Opening them up, she turned to me and said, "I don't loan my books out to anybody, Javier."

I nodded my head, not sure what she was getting at.

"You may choose some books to borrow for the break, if you'd like."

I browsed for a while, then chose five.

"Now I'll choose some books that I think you'll enjoy," she said, and then quickly pulled out five more. With each book she pulled out, she sighed and muttered, "Ohhh, this is good," like she was eating a really good piece of cake or something. When she was done, she closed her cabinets and told me to have a nice holiday. I thanked her and started for the door.

"And Javier . . ."

I turned around to face her. She had the same look my mom gets when I leave for school in the morning and she wants me to be careful on the streets.

"Yeah?"

"Don't steal anything while you're on break. Remember, it's a dangerous habit."

"Yeah. I heard you the first time."

So that first Monday of the break, I pulled out the books she had picked for me, figuring those would be the boring ones. I'd read hers first and save the best for last. But as I started to read Edna Ferber's *So Big*, I discovered that Mrs. Aronson had pretty good taste when it came to books. I loved books that had farms and the frontier in them, and this one had both. I wondered about High Prairie, the town in the book, and if there ever really was a place like that.

I read for three hours straight and was halfway through the book when the phone rang. It was Jesse. He was bored and wanted to walk to the convenience store for a soda. After getting dressed, I called my mom at work to tell her I was leaving and then took off.

Jesse was waiting for me on the corner. He had a smile on his face when he saw me coming down the street, which meant he was probably high.

"What up, G?" he called out to me.

We started walking.

"You see Eduardo?" I asked him.

"I stopped by his house when I left mine. His mom said he took off with Desi this morning. They're probably at Ruby's."

"How's your vacation going?"

"Shit. My brother's babies are all over the house. Dirty diapers and milk bottles everywhere. Crying and all that shit. Can't game. Can't read. Can't smoke. I had to get out of there."

I started laughing as I thought of all that stuff going on and poor Jesse trying to find a hiding place to smoke his herb. When he heard me laughing, he chuckled too.

At the convenience store I could tell Jesse was in no hurry to get back home. He hung around to browse at the magazines, and when the attendant turned his back to us, he stashed a girlie magazine in his jacket. From the other side of the aisle, I smiled to him. It was funny when Jesse was bad, because I guess it messed with his whole image of being smart and maybe even becoming a priest some day. When we got to the counter with our sodas, he pulled out a twenty and paid for both of us. I was shocked, 'cause Jesse never did stuff like that. Eduardo and Desi would, since they were doing stuff for the Playaz now, but Jesse never had that kind of money before. While the attendant was ringing up the sale Jesse noticed a display of candy bars right in front of us. Quickly he gave me the eye to boost a couple. I eyed the attendant and timed his motions. Just as I was about to grab the candy, Mrs. Aronson's words suddenly crossed my mind: "Javier. Don't steal anything while you're on break. Remember, it's a dangerous habit." *Shit*, I thought, and reluctantly stuffed my free hand back into my pocket.

When we got outside, Jesse let me have it.

"What was up with that?"

"What?"

"How come you didn't get the candy?"

"The guy would've caught me. I'm Jonah, remember? Even you said so!"

"No way. You had him beat."

"Why didn't you just pay for it? You had the money."

" 'Cause we coulda had the money *and* the candy."

"Shit, no. I would've got caught. And where'd you get that money from anyway?"

Jesse didn't say anything. Surprised that the question had shut him up so suddenly, I said it again, and still nothing.

We walked along for a while in silence. I didn't know what to say, but I knew something was up with the money. Jesse had never in his life given me the silent treatment, even if he was mad at me. After a couple of minutes, he finally spoke up.

"Eduardo gave me the money."

"For what?"

"Just for friends. I guess he's making a lot of cash doing

what he's doing. I ran into him on Saturday, and he threw forty bucks at me like it was nothing. 'If you go somewhere, treat Javier,' he said."

When Jesse said that, I wanted to hide under a rock. It's one thing to be poor, but it's another thing to be poor and have your friends plot to treat you for stuff.

"And check this out. He gave me a gun to hide for him too," Jesse added.

"No shit! What'd you do with it?"

"Hid it where my brothers hide their guns."

For some reason, that made me laugh, thinking that Jesse had guns he was hiding for all these hoods. His brothers were locked up in the pen already, and from the sound of it, Eduardo and Desi were on their way there. I guess Jesse started to see the humor in it too, so he started laughing.

Between chuckles I asked, "What happened to you, man? You were supposed to be a priest! Look at you now!" I pulled the girlie magazine out of his jacket and shoved it in his face. "Look at you now!"

Jesse and I laughed hard. Just then a car pulled up beside us. Desi stuck his head out the back window and shouted out, "Homeboys!"

Eduardo was sitting in the front passenger seat and Ruby was driving. Desi was sitting in back next to a car seat carrying Ruby's baby.

"Hey, what's up?" Desi asked.

"Rolling back to Ruby's. We're gonna game! You down?" Eduardo asked.

Waiting to hear Jesse's excuse before I gave mine, I hung back while he spoke up first.

"Told my mom I'd back in an hour. I can't."

"Same," I replied.

"Cool. You know where we're at!" Eduardo said, and then they sped off.

By the time I got back home, I'd missed Springer, so I started back in on the Ferber book. I read all the way to six o'clock and I finished it, and then I made dinner. As soon as my ramen came out of the microwave the phone rang. It was Jessica. She was all psyched about our project and how cool it was starting to come out. While she talked, I ate.

"I found so many pictures online that our project might run like ten minutes if we use them all!"

"Uh-huh," I replied with a mouth full of noodles.

"I even found some videos of hippies and the Vietnam War and stuff on an archive site."

"Cool."

"You should come over and look at it."

I swallowed hard on the food I was chewing.

"At your house?"

"Duh! Yeah, at my house. My dad's home all week. He's cool. He doesn't care if we work on our project here."

"Oh. Yeah, okay."

"Tomorrow afternoon then."

"Okay."

Jessica gave me directions, then hung up. For a while I just sat there and wondered what it all meant. This might look like we were boyfriend and girlfriend or something. If anybody at school knew about it, that's what they'd think.

Because I hadn't even started working on my end of the project, the narration part, I got out the articles that Jessica had given to me and started writing. By the time my mom got home at eleven, I had two and a half pages of dialogue. I told my mom about working over at Jessica's the next day, but she didn't seem too cool about it. She asked me a lot of questions about her. Who was she? Where did she live? What did her parents do? All that stuff. I started thinking that she wasn't going to let me go, until I mentioned that her dad was in the military. And for some reason that made everything all right.

"Really, the military?" she asked, like I was lying about it or something.

"Yeah. He's like a helicopter pilot."

"Oh. Well, I guess it's all right. Just be careful walking up there, and be home before it gets dark."

"All right."

My mom still made me give her the directions to Jessica's house and her phone number and stuff, but she was letting me go, so I didn't care.

The next morning after my mom left for work, I tried to start another one of the books Mrs. Aronson loaned me, but I was too nervous to concentrate. I kept thinking about going over to Jessica's and what it would be like. I'd never been over to a girl's house before. I wasn't sure how to act or anything. It would be different if all the guys were going with me, because then I could rely on Eduardo to do all the talking and stuff. But it was going to be just me and her and her dad.

I had to leave early because Jessica lived on the Northside near the country club, where all the other rich people in my town lived. It was probably going to take me forty-five minutes just to walk there. As I thought about it, I considered calling up Eduardo to see if Ruby could give me a lift, but then I figured they'd want me to go back to Ruby's after to hang out, and I'd be put on the spot.

I took off by noon and headed up Canyon Avenue, and then

made a left on Sage Brush and a right on Coyote Avenue. That was the easy walk. The hard part was walking all the way up Coyote to the Northside. It was probably two or three miles and it felt like forever.

When I finally made it to the Northside, I reached Jessica's street in a new housing tract. All the houses looked alike. They were two stories with tan-colored stucco and tile roofs. All the homes had three-car garages, and some of them had really nice cars in their driveways. Jessica's house was easy to find 'cause her pop's Hummer stood out like a ship on dry land.

Jessica answered right away when I rang the bell. Swinging open the door, she seemed all hyper and excited. She was barefoot, and even her toenails were painted black. I could smell coffee and cigarettes on her breath.

"Javier–Twentieth Century! Come in! I'm working in the dining room," she said.

The house was big, too big for just two people. The floors were all wood and tile. There was hardly any furniture, and there were no pictures on the walls. I wondered if all white people's houses looked like that.

Jessica hopped across the dining room and landed on a chair at the dining room table, facing a real flashy looking laptop. There was a coffee cup beside it. That explained why she was so hyper. I took off my coat and sat down in a chair beside her.

"Look at this stuff," she said as she spun the laptop around so I could see the screen.

There was some video playing of the Vietnam War, with soldiers smoking and shooting machine guns and stuff.

"Cool," I said, nodding my head.

"And there's more! I'm finding all kinds of stuff. Our project is going to rock!"

I had my narration pages folded up in my pocket, so I took them out and showed them to her. She read them silently and nodded. For a second I thought about Dontae because of the way she was nodding. Just then, a white guy with a shaved head walked into the room. He held a coffee cup and looked real serious.

"Go away, Dad," Jessica said without looking up.

Jessica's dad walked over to me with an outstretched hand. I shook it. He had a really strong grip and a look in his eyes that I'd seen before. He didn't like Mexican people. His eyes said, "I don't like you, but I'm trying to be mature about this."

"Hi. My name's Casey."

"Javier."

"So you're working on a project with Jessica?"

"Yeah. She's my partner."

"Cool. Want something to drink?"

Jessica piped up with, "Bring him some coffee, Dad."

I didn't want to disagree with Jessica, even though I didn't like coffee, so I nodded.

"One coffee coming up. Sugar? Cream?"

"Just black with sugar, Dad," Jessica said for me.

I nodded again, and Casey went off to get the coffee.

Jessica and I started working, and it was kind of fun, except that she was so extreme. She thought fast, and sometimes she could be thinking about something totally different from what she was saying. It was like everything she did was a chess game and she was five or six moves ahead of herself. I was right in thinking that she was smarter than Jesse. It seemed like she knew something about everything, and what she didn't know, she'd figure out in a few seconds. No wonder she didn't do very well in school. With her kind of mind, school probably drove her nuts. Every now and then she'd say she had to use the bathroom. And when she left, I'd hear the back door of the house opening and closing. A few minutes later she'd come back in and sit down smelling like cigarettes.

"Your dad's not going to bust you?" I asked after her second smoke break.

"I get busted all the time. It's not like I go anywhere anyway. Being grounded is the same as not being grounded. He'll take my phone, though, if he's pissed."

"How come you smoke?"

"I've been doing it since we lived in Germany. It's no big deal over there. Over here it's like a criminal act or something."

I started to laugh 'cause Jessica was so off-the-wall.

We had a good time working that afternoon, but I was relieved when it was time for me to go home because I was so tired. Before I walked out the door, she gave me a hug. It was the first time a girl had ever given me a hug. I didn't know what to do, so I tried to act like it was no big deal. But I couldn't wait to get home so I could call Jesse.

Back on the streets I hustled because it was five o'clock already. It'd be dark in forty-five minutes or so, and I'd promised my mom I'd be home before then. I was still on Jessica's street making my way back to Sage Brush Avenue when I saw a few kids approaching me from the other direction. They looked about my age and were wearing white T-shirts and baggies. There were three of them, and they were goofing, so I didn't stress over them. If they said anything to me, I'd just say I was a Northsider. They couldn't know every kid on the Northside. As we got closer to each other I walked faster, like I had somewhere to be. At ten feet away I could see two of them weren't paying attention to me at all, but one of them was kind of staring. Then he did it. He nudged another, and that one nudged the next. They studied me as we were about to pass each other. Then one called out, "Yo! Hey!"

I kept walking like they weren't talking to me.

"Hey!"

I stepped off the sidewalk and down into the gutter to pass them when one turned around.

"Hey!" one called out again.

I had to turn to face him. If I didn't, it might have been worse for me.

"Yeah?"

"What set you claim?"

"Northside," I mumbled out.

"What?" one asked.

"Northside," I repeated.

"What school you go to?" another one asked.

I didn't know any schools on the Northside, so I didn't know what to say.

One of the kids looked me over from head to toe, and then asked, "How come you got Chuck T's on if you're a Northsider?"

I'd completely forgotten that Northsiders didn't wear Chuck T's. They wore white leather Conquerors. Dumbfounded, I looked down to my shoes to stall. I looked up just in time to see a fist flying toward my face. BAMMM! My head snapped back, and then another fist nailed me across my jaw. All I could see was a haze of white T-shirts and fists. I coughed and felt like throwing up as another punch nailed me square in the stomach, and I went down. Again and again I felt punches hitting me all over.

Suddenly I heard a horn blast. A kick came from behind and drilled me right between my shoulder blades. Then I heard footsteps running and an engine nearby. My vision was fuzzy, but I thought I could see Casey looking me over. I blinked until my eyes cleared enough to register the puzzled look on his face.

"Javier! Javier!"

"I'm all right" came out of my mouth.

Casey helped me onto my feet and walked me to the Hummer. As I climbed up into the truck my head started to clear. Licking my lips, I tasted blood. Then one at a time, my jaw, then my stomach, then my lips began to throb with pain.

Casey hopped into the driver's seat of the Hummer and just looked at me for a while.

"You want to call the cops? The kids all scattered when I hit the horn."

"No, I'm cool."

"Anything broken?"

"Nah, I'm cool. Just want to go home."

I didn't want Casey to see our apartment, so I gave him directions to the front of Jesse's house. When we got there, I was glad Jesse and Eduardo were out front dribbling a soccer ball. They stopped playing when they saw the Hummer pull up.

"You sure you're okay?"

"Yeah, I'm all right. My mom will fix me up."

"Okay. You're lucky I decided to go to the market or who knows what would've happened."

"Yeah. Thanks," I said, and then stepped out of the truck. I watched until Casey pulled off.

"WHAT THE FUCK?" Eduardo called out.

I walked over to the guys. They looked surprised to see me all tore up.

"What happened to you?" Jesse asked.

"Got jumped by some Northsiders."

"No shit!" Eduardo shouted.

Jesse ran into his house and brought me out a soda. As I stood there with the guys staring at me I wanted to cry. Right then and there, I felt so fed up with the whole Playaz and Northsiders thing, the whole being poor thing, the fact that my dad was in jail, and the fact that I couldn't do anything about any of it, that I just felt done with it all. My breath got tight, and I felt a cry coming on, but I fought it. Even if they were my homies, I couldn't let them see me looking like a punk. I drank down the soda and tried to pretend it was no big deal as they kept asking me questions.

"How many?" Jesse asked.

"Three."

"Do you know them?" Eduardo quizzed.

"No."

"What were you doing up there?" asked Jesse.

"I was working on a school project with Jessica."

"Shiittt," Eduardo sang. "The shit's going down! If they wanna fuck with my homies, they're fucked! That's all I got to say about it."

"Don't say anything to anybody. I don't want to look like a punk."

"Fuck that!" Eduardo shrugged off my words.

"No, really, man. I'll look like a punk if word gets out I got jumped. Don't say anything. Come on. Promise?"

"I don't know," Eduardo replied.

"I'm going home," I said as I finished up the soda. I handed the empty can to Jesse and walked off.

Back home in front of the bathroom mirror, I saw for myself why the guys were staring in disbelief. I looked like hell. I had a fat lip, a black eye, puffy cheeks, and cuts on my face. Thank God it was Thanksgiving break and I didn't have to go to school the next day looking like that.

After cleaning myself up as best I could, I crashed out on the couch in the front room. I turned on the TV, propped my feet up, and looked at my Chuck T's. They were wearing out. Suddenly I thought of what Mrs. Aronson said about stealing. She was right again. The shoes I'd stolen turned out to be the thing that blew my cover and got my ass kicked. And my day was far from over. My mom would be home later, and she was going to freak for sure when she saw me.

"Shit." I kicked off my shoes and threw them across the room.

# CHAPTER 11

By Thanksgiving Day, Mom was just starting to cool off about me getting jumped. When she'd found out about it two nights before, she'd come down on me like it was my fault, but on Thanksgiving she seemed to let it go. She was happy 'cause she only worked a short day shift at work. Then she came home and made Thanksgiving dinner for us. We'd gotten invited over to both my abuelas' houses for the holiday, but my mom didn't like either one, not even her own mom, so she made dinner at the apartment instead. We had turkey stuffed with rice, mashed potatoes and gravy, cranberry sauce, and pumpkin pie. It was a nice dinner, but I couldn't stop thinking about my pop. If he'd just managed to stay out a few weeks more, he could've been with us. He would've loved all the food.

For the rest of my vacation, I read. I mowed through seven books, and by the time Monday came, I was glad I was going back to school so I could find something new. When I walked into Mrs. McHalenn's for first period, I guess it showed.

"Oh, my goodness!" she said dramatically. "Javier is here and he's actually smiling! Somebody must've had a good holiday."

I just ignored her and sat down at my desk. I'm sure my

smile changed minutes later when she handed back a test we'd taken right before break. There were checks all over the paper and a big red D on the top.

Jessica brought in her laptop for Mr. O'Neil's class so we could edit our video during project session. She asked me what had happened that afternoon when I walked home from her house, but I didn't want to say anything about it. The last thing a guy wants to tell a girl is how he got his ass kicked. That day she started to sit right next to me while we worked, instead of across from me, and she kept leaning on me. I wasn't sure if that meant anything 'cause I'd never had a girlfriend before. I figured I'd ask Jesse about it later to see if it was a signal or something. He'd never had a girlfriend either, but he might know about stuff like that from his brothers.

When I got to Mrs. Aronson's class, it was like a big party. Everybody was happy to be back. Mrs. Aronson was smiling from ear to ear. I guess she had a good time with her family back East. Mrs. Aronson brought everybody back a present from New York. Some of the kids got key chains, others got T-shirts with NEW YORK splashed across them, and the teacher's aide and I each got a bag of what looked like doughnuts but were stiff rolls instead.

"What are they?" I asked Mrs. Aronson, opening the bag.

"They're bagels. You eat 'em. They're the best kind. You can't find these out here in California. You put butter on them, or jelly, or cream cheese. I like mine with peanut butter."

"Oh. Thanks," I said, not too sure that I was going to like them.

Dontae got a T-shirt, and he seemed hypnotized by it. He cradled it while sitting in his wheelchair, and fingered the lettering. He only looked up from it when I sat down at his desk to start working.

Seeing me, he called out, "Read!"

He had finished up his morning work, so I pulled the *Islands* book out of my backpack and started right in where we left off. I never thought I'd admit it, but it was nice to be back at school.

That afternoon I walked home with Jesse. I still had the whole Jessica thing on my mind, so I asked him about it.

"She wants you, man!" he cried out after hearing my story.

"What?"

"She wants you."

"Just 'cause she sat next to me and leaned on me?"

"There's this thing called body language, man. And usually it's little signals and gestures and stuff that tells you if somebody likes you or not. But when it's actual contact, there's no question. Like it or not, you gotta girlfriend!"

"No way!"

"Yes way! Just don't get all gothy and stuff."

"Well, I don't know if I even like her."

"Doesn't matter. She picked you. That's the way it goes. Just ride it out and see what happens."

"Whatever."

My mom had gotten off early from work, so she was home when I got home. I showed her the bagels that Mrs. Aronson had given me.

"They're good. It's Jewish food," she said on seeing them.

"Really?"

"Yeah. You're teacher's Jewish?"

"I don't know," I said with a shrug. I wasn't sure what Mrs. Aronson was. I always just thought she was a white lady. I had read the *Chosen* book she'd lent me the week before, so I knew a little bit about Jewish people. They had these rules they had to follow about food and the Sabbath.

My mom toasted a bagel and put some butter on it. I tasted it, and it was tough and chewy. It wasn't bad, but it wasn't all that good either.

So things were going pretty smooth. I got back into my routine at school, and Jesse had been right when he said that Jessica and I were pretty much boyfriend and girlfriend. And Christmas was coming up. But there was stuff going on in the background that I didn't know about, stuff that was about to get real hard-core.

It was a Wednesday afternoon and I was home alone, reading after school, when I heard someone running up the steps to the apartment. I threw down my book and jumped over to the window. Jesse was running up the stairs like his life depended on it. I threw open the front door, my heart flipping around in my chest. He was hunched over and out of breath, beads of sweat all over his face. With his hands on his knees, he looked up to me.

"You're not gonna believe it," he said, huffing and puffing.

"Come in," I invited.

"No! I need some herb. Outside in the alley."

I grabbed my jacket, and we went around the building so Jesse could smoke without being seen. Leaning up against the trash bin, he packed his pipe.

"Hurry, man! What happened?" I asked.

"You're not going to believe it," he said again as he lit his pipe. He took a big drag, and started hacking and coughing, his face all red. I felt sad to see him like that, but I didn't know what to say or how to say it.

Jesse took a couple of more drags before he settled down enough to get to the point. Then out it came.

"Eduardo and Desi got popped by the cops," he said, deflating as the news was finally out.

"No shit?"

"No shit!"

"What happened?"

Jesse hit the pipe again, took a deep drag, and exhaled.

"They were rolling around the Northside. They jumped some bangers."

I couldn't believe it.

"What happened?"

"They whupped some kids right into the hospital."

"Why'd they do it?"

"Everything. The Halloween drive-by, you getting jumped, just everything."

"If they got popped, they're going down."

"I know," Jesse agreed.

"Who told them to do it?"

"Nobody. They were flying solo."

"Well then, the homies are going to spank them for that."

"I know."

When Jesse was calm enough, we went back around to the front of the apartments and sat on the steps. He told me the whole story with details. I hadn't known it at the time, but Eduardo and Desi were hot to prove to the Playaz that they were down for theirs. Ever since they'd gotten out of juvie, they'd liked all the attention and power they were getting, so they played it for more. Since Roberto was locked up, all those little jobs fell into their laps. They were doing runs for the gang all over the valley. They were meeting all the honchos and shot callers. All kinds of scandalous dudes would hang out at Ruby's for whatever reason, so Eduardo and Desi were making contacts. From the details that Jesse was giving me, I wasn't surprised at how it all turned out.

Ever since the drive-by, Eduardo and Desi had been plotting what they could to do for payback. They weren't even going to get an okay from the head honchos. They were just going to do it and then get the credit for the payback, which they guessed was going to be praise. Then when I got jumped during Thanksgiving break, they had an extra reason to do what they were going to do because I was one of their best homies. So every day after school, after their runs around town for the Playaz, they were cruising the Northside on the down low, spying for some kids to jump. They weren't just going to jump any old random kids. They were looking for true Northsiders with white tees, baggies, and Conquerors.

So yesterday afternoon at around five thirty, they'd found just what they were looking for. There were two Northsiders at a park up there, hanging out. They looked like they were middle schoolers, so the guys had Ruby park the car on the street. Then they hopped out and bumrushed them. Immediately they threw them down and started beating on them. When Eduardo and Desi had those two whupped, they got up, went back to the car, and took off.

Back at Ruby's, they were sipping beer, gaming, and talking trash about how well they'd done when all of sudden Child Protective Services busted in for an inspection on Ruby. They saw all the beer cans. They smelled herb burning. The apartment was a mess. The baby was in a dirty diaper. So they hauled all of them downtown. While Eduardo and Desi were waiting for their parents to pick them up, some county deputy sheriff walked by to turn in some paperwork and noticed that they fit the description of two juveniles who'd just beaten up some kids. He'd taken the report himself. He looked at Eduardo's and Desi's skinned knuckles. Just like that, he put two and two together. Now the Northsiders' parents were claiming that their kids didn't even belong to a gang, so they were gonna press full charges. Bail was set, but neither Desi's nor Eduardo's folks could swing it. The guys will be stuck in juvie until trial, and with the positive IDs they got from the kids that they beat up, they're most likely going to YA for at least six months.

Over and over again, Jesse and I muttered, "Shit!"

Our friends were pinched, and there was a good chance we wouldn't see them for a long time. Just then, sitting with Jesse on the steps of the apartment building, I was glad I was who I was. If that was a geek or a coward or a punk or whatever, I was glad. I wasn't in juvie. Sure, Eduardo and Desi were my best friends in the world, but I didn't want to be in their shoes. I didn't say anything to Jesse, but again I got the sense that stoned and all, he was thinking the exact same thing.

After a while Jesse got up, threw his hand out to shake mine, and left. I sat there on the steps by myself for a while before going inside. I just wanted to breathe the fresh air. It scared me that from now on, Eduardo and Desi couldn't come and go when they wanted to. Even though we were kids and had to do the things we were told to do, we could still go outside or walk home from school or do whatever. We were free. And I wanted to keep feeling that because I could.

The rest of that week, I guess I was in shock. Only Jesse might have known how I really felt. As for the rest of the people

I ran into, I didn't usually say much to them anyway, so I didn't think they'd see a change in me. Jessica said something about me not being myself, but I played it off like I had a lot of stuff to do. I reached Friday and figured I was good for the weekend, but then Friday turned out to be more intense than Wednesday could have ever been.

When I finally made it to Mrs. Aronson's room, it seemed like the heaviest weight I'd carried in my life slipped off my shoulders. It was like her classroom had become my life raft. As soon as I walked in, I noticed Dontae was there, and I felt better on the spot. Dontae noticed me right off the bat.

"Read!" he said hoarsely, like he'd had a rough morning already.

I took off my backpack and jacket and went over to his table. He still had to finish up some math from the morning, so I sat down and started helping him with it. I'd been there like ten minutes when I realized something seemed wrong with Dontae. His face was redder than usual, like he'd been outside on a really cold day. Not thinking it meant much, I just kept going on with his work.

After about twenty minutes we finally got to read. We only had about twenty pages left in the *Islands* book, and I was eager to see how it was going to end.

Again Dontae called out, "Read!" when he saw me take the book out.

I began reading like normal, and Dontae went into his usual listening trance. But this time, it was different. I'd gone on for a couple of minutes when Dontae started clearing his throat and coughing every now and then. Then he was sweating just sitting there in his wheelchair. That didn't seem natural to me. All of a sudden, he started coughing and couldn't seem to stop.

"Dontae?" I said, trying to get his attention.

He kept his eyes closed like he was still listening to me read while coughing.

"Dontae? You want some water?" I tried again. Nothing happened. He stayed the way he was, still hacking.

Something wasn't right at all, so I called Mrs. Aronson over.

"He's coughing. A lot. It's like he can't breathe," I told her.

Mrs. Aronson quickly put her hand on Dontae's forehead.

"He's hot," she replied.

She put her hand to Dontae's face. "Dontae! Dontae! Open your eyes, Dontae!"

Dontae kept coughing, and at one big cough his eyes popped open. He looked totally surprised, like he wasn't sure why he was coughing, but he couldn't stop. Then Mrs. Aronson tried to straighten him up in his chair 'cause he was all slouched over, but the coughing got worse. His face was red, and he was sweating more than ever.

Coolly Mrs. Aronson called out to the teacher's aide, "Get the nurse!"

The aide jumped to the phone and made the call. Mrs. Aronson kept trying to straighten Dontae out, I guess so he could breathe better. She checked his pulse, then reclined the wheelchair so he was lying back a little.

In no time at all, the nurse trotted into the room carrying a big red emergency bag. She seemed in control when she arrived, like she could handle anything. She looked Dontae over, felt his pulse, and looked into his eyes. And the whole time Dontae coughed. Dribbles of phlegm were on the corners of his mouth. The nurse grew graver, then she said it.

"Sounds like his lungs have fluid in them. Code White! Call nine-one-one!"

And just like that, the situation got intense for real.

Mrs. Aronson rushed to the phone and made a call to the office. She didn't go into details. The only words she said were "Code White! Call nine-one-one!"

"Javier? Could you help me get the other students set up in the kitchen?" the aide asked me.

I nodded yes, and then following the aide's lead, I helped guide the other students to the kitchen table. She brought out snacks to keep them occupied.

I guessed the teachers and nurses had trained for this 'cause they moved like clockwork. Mrs. Aronson cleared a path for the paramedics while the nurse tried to lean Dontae on his side so he could breathe easier. Then Mrs. Aronson called Dontae's mom. She sounded more serious and sadder than I'd ever heard her before.

"Hi, Mrs. Johnson. This is Dontae's teacher, Rachel Aronson. Yes. Dontae's having a coughing fit, so we're taking him to the hospital right now. I'll meet you there. Bye now," she said, then hung up. Catching a glimpse of me, she motioned for me to stay with the other students.

A few minutes passed, then in came like twenty people. The principal, the vice-principal, and school security guards, all rushed in following six paramedics with a stretcher. The paramedics carried these huge black cases that looked heavy and full. They set right to work on Dontae. There were so many people around him, I couldn't even really see what they were doing, but I heard them say Dontae had a temperature of

103. As dumb as I was about medical things, I still knew that was serious.

Even with his temperature and all that coughing, I still didn't believe Dontae could be that bad . . . well, at least I *hoped* he wasn't all that bad. After a while the paramedics got him onto the stretcher and strapped him down. They put an IV in his arm, and he still had that look of surprise on his face like before. He must've been scared. I would've been if I'd been in his shoes. Eventually they wheeled Dontae out of the classroom, and Mrs. Aronson grabbed her purse and coat and followed them. For a while the principal and vice-principal hung around the classroom, quietly whispering to each other. And then of all people, Mr. O'Neil rushed in. He was carrying a bagged lunch, and it looked like he'd just been eating. I guessed he was supposed to cover for Mrs. Aronson 'cause he sat right down at her desk and made himself comfortable. He waved over to me.

"Aren't you late for lunch, Javier?"

I looked at the clock and saw I'd already missed twenty minutes of it. I hadn't even thought about eating with all that was going on. By the time I got my backpack and jacket and made it out the door, I'd missed lunch completely, so I headed to math.

On our walk home from school that day, Jesse wanted to know all about what happened. I guess the Dontae thing had just added to my shock about Eduardo and Desi 'cause I found it hard to talk that afternoon. He kept prodding me for details and stuff, but I just couldn't say much. Maybe it was starting to sink in that in the past three days, I'd lost three of my friends.

When I got home that afternoon, Jessica called me. She wanted to know what happened in Mrs. Aronson's too. When

I saw her in our math and science classes after it happened, I'd said I'd tell her later. By the time I talked to her that night, I didn't mind telling her everything. She got a better version than Jesse. I got the feeling that Jessica kind of wished that she been there to see everything. Maybe she was an adrenaline freak or something.

"Dammnn! No way!" she sighed over the phone. "That's better than anything on TV!"

"I guess," I replied.

"So you think he's going to be all right?"

"I don't know. When I have a cold, I'm always better in like two or three days."

"Kids like him have other conditions," she explained.

"Like what?"

"I don't know. I just know they sometimes have other conditions that you can't see. Sometimes their systems are weaker."

"How do you know that?"

"I just know. Maybe I saw it on TV or something."

Hearing Jessica say that really made me stress out over Dontae. I hadn't been too worried about him back in the classroom 'cause I thought that if he had a cold, he'd get over it like everybody else. But then I started to wonder, what if he didn't? What if he was all messed up inside? What if he was dead?

My mom got home at about eight that night. It was early for her. I was watching TV, and as soon as she came through the door, the phone rang. She started talking in her customer service voice, so I knew it was somebody official. I heard her say a couple of times, "Okay, I'll tell him," so I knew it was about me too. When she got off the line, she told me the news.

"That was your teacher, Mrs. Aronson. She's still at the

hospital with the kid you tutor. She wanted me to tell you that Dontae is really sick, so he's staying in the hospital. She said don't worry, they're watching him real close. She said she'll see you Monday."

Jessica had been right. It was worse than I expected.

# CHAPTER 12

My mom knew I was worried about Dontae. I could see it in the way she looked at me.

"You two close?" she asked.

"He's my friend."

"Just a part of growing up. People we know and care about get sick. Sometimes they even die. That's just life. Praying helps, you know. Say one for him."

"Yeah. I will," I replied.

Since my mom started going to her prayer group to get off the speed, she'd been bringing up prayer a lot around me. I was glad it was working for her, and I really wanted to tell her, but I didn't want to stress her out now that she was straight, so I had to pick my words carefully.

"You're doing really good with the prayer group thing," I said nonchalantly.

She turned from the clothes she was folding on the couch to look at me.

"I didn't think you noticed."

"I noticed. I just didn't want to get you all stressed out."

"Well, thank you. Now give me hug."

I did, and it felt good. Not just the hug, but being honest. I was glad she knew I was proud of her.

The weekend seemed to last forever. I could barely sleep or eat or do anything. My mom was crashed out sleeping most of the time, not because of speed, but because she had worked so many hours that week. Because Dontae was on my mind, all I could do was pace from the front room into my bedroom over and over again. Then I'd turn the TV on, search the channels, and turn it off. I'd pick up a book, start reading, then lose my place. I'd warm a burrito in the microwave and end up leaving it untouched. On Saturday night Jessica called me up. I was going bonkers just being by myself, so I was glad she called, but I played it cool. She didn't really have anything to say. I guess she was bored and just wanted to be in contact with somebody. And even though we didn't say much to each other, we kept one another on the phone. Every now and then one of us would say something.

"So you heard anything about Dontae?" she asked.

"Nah, just that he's really, really sick and still in the hospital."

"Damn. That's sad."

"How's our project?" I asked her.

"Cool. Just taking a break. Ours is going to be the best. I saw what some other kids were doing. Nobody's doing a video but us. We got 'em beat!"

And then from out of nowhere, Jessica threw me for a loop.

"We should go to the movies tomorrow," she said, like it was the most ordinary thing that should happen on a Sunday.

"Huh?"

"The movies. Don't tell me you've never been to the movies, Javier–Twentieth Century!"

"Of course I've been to the movies."

"Well, then. Come on. I'll have my dad take us."

I thought of Casey, her dad, and that I-don't-like-Mexicans look in his eyes. Doing a school project was one thing, but going out with his daughter was another. I got the feeling he probably wouldn't be too cool with it. Instead of me saying no to her, I figured I'd let him do it for me. That way I wouldn't have to go through with the whole thing.

"Yeah. Okay. I'll go."

I gave Jessica directions to Jesse's house, and she said she'd be there by two. After hanging up the phone with her, I called Jesse. I could hear a video game in the background.

"Hey."

"What's up?" he replied.

"You still got some of that money Eduardo gave you?"

"Yeah, some. Why?"

"Jessica wants to go to the movies, and I don't have any cash."

"The goth-gringa? Ha! I told yoouuu!" he sang.

"Shut up, man. So it's down?"

"Yeah. I got it."

"I'll be over tomorrow. They're gonna pick me up over there."

"Here?"

"Yeah."

"Why?"

"I don't want her to see the apartments."

"Okay. Cool. See you tomorrow."

Even though I set up the plan with Jesse, I wasn't really thinking she'd show up. But just in case she did, I didn't want her pop to see my street with all the broken-down cars, and apartments with dingy paint, and beer bottles in the gutters. Jesse's street wasn't much better, but they had a house with a neat lawn out front. I figured that might look nicer to Jessica's pop.

That night, after I went to bed, I couldn't sleep. What if she actually *did* show up? What was I supposed to do? How was I supposed to act? Then when I was thinking about that, I wondered about Dontae. Was he okay? From what Jessica had mentioned the day before, he might be dying for all I knew. He was the reason why I felt like going to school at all. If he wasn't there, what would I have?

Eventually I did drift off to sleep. I woke up late Sunday morning 'cause Mom was crashed out too. It was maybe ten when I got out of bed. And already I was wondering what I should wear that afternoon. I didn't have a lot of clothes. The most I had were maybe four shirts and four pairs of pants, so I tried to pick out the neatest ones. I took a bath and everything, then got dressed.

My mom was up by the time I got out of the bathroom. She could tell I was nervous.

"What's up with you?"

"Got a date."

"A date? With who?"

"That girl I'm doing my project with."

"Really?" she said with a smile.

"Really."

"Oh. Well, excuse me."

She grinned as she sat on the couch watching TV while I scurried around trying to look decent. By one o'clock I looked neater than I had ever looked in my life. I'd touched up my shaved head and clipped my nails and everything. I'd even put on some of my pop's spiced aftershave.

"Where are you going?" my mom asked when I was ready to leave.

"Movies."

"You need money?"

I knew money was tight, and I didn't want my mom to feel guilty about it, so I lied.

"We got free passes from Halloween."

"Oh. You sure?"

"Yeah, I'm sure."

And with that I grabbed my jacket, and was out the door.

I was early, so I took my time getting to Jesse's. Jessica hadn't called to tell me that the date was off, like I had figured she would. That meant that she just might show up. Then I'd have to go on the date. A real date, with a girl.

By the time I made it to Jesse's, I felt weak and dizzy. Jesse was outside waiting for me and started laughing when he saw me coming down the sidewalk.

"Goth-boy!" he yelled out.

I smiled because it was kind of funny. Jesse came through with twenty bucks. It was all he had left of the money Eduardo gave him. I didn't know how much a movie and stuff would cost, but I told him it was fine. We sat on the porch of his house and waited for Jessica to arrive.

"You nervous?" Jesse asked.

"A little."

"Want to get high?" he said, then started laughing.

Eventually the Hummer pulled up in front of the house. Jessica jumped out of the passenger seat, opened the door to the back, and waved excitedly for me to hop in. I shook hands with Jesse and then started walking to the truck.

Joking, Jesse called out, "Hey, homie! Don't become a vampire!"

I wanted to laugh, but I was too nervous even to smile.

Jessica hopped into the backseat next to me, and we took off. Casey said hi and I said hi back, but that was it. I started to get the impression that Jessica was in charge of her pop. She held the remote to the stereo and started playing some Slipknot. She played it loud and started rocking out.

"You like this?" she yelled over to me with a smile.

I shook my head no, and her smile flattened.

"Oh. Well, what do you like?"

I never really listened to music much, so I thought of what the rest of the homies would say if they were in the same situation.

"Oldies."

"Oldies? I don't have any oldies. Maybe my dad does. Hey, Dad? You have any oldies?"

"Like what?" Casey replied, dropping his sun visor which carried CDs.

"I don't know, oldies! What do you have?"

Looking up to his visor, Casey answered, "I have the Allman Brothers, the Eagles, Pink Floyd."

Jessica looked at me to see if I liked any of them. I'd never heard of any of those groups, so I shook my head again.

"Just put in some Beatles then, Dad," Jessica commanded decisively.

For a while I was able to forget everything that was going down. Jessica had an energy that sucked you in. As we rode to the movies she showed me pictures on her phone. She'd show me one, and before I could see it, she'd be thumbing to the next one. Then Latrice would text her, and she'd fire off a message back. She could probably text faster than a secretary could type.

When we got to the theater, I was glad Casey had come with us. Tickets for the movie were thirty dollars for the three of us! I knew they were going to be expensive, but I thought I'd have enough for our tickets and some popcorn. Before I could even reach in my pocket for the twenty Jesse had given me, Casey whipped out his credit card and paid. He did the same for the popcorn and drinks, which were another thirty bucks. Jessica wanted some licorice on top of that, so eight more dollars went on the bill. The total for everything before we even sat down was sixty-eight dollars. There'd be no way I could even mention spending that kind of money to my mom, but Casey paid like it was nothing.

Jessica was a big fan of action movies. Even though there was a big vampire movie out that I thought she'd want to see, she insisted on Jackie Chan. While hanging out with her, I started to learn that for her everything was a story about somewhere in the world she had lived. When it came to movies, she explained how in most parts of the world, action adventures were the most popular 'cause you didn't need to know what they were saying. Action was the universal language. I shrugged and nodded.

The theater was just about empty, so we picked seats up front. Casey sat behind us. I didn't want to turn around to see that look in his eyes, so I kept mine on the screen.

The movie was good and I got into it right away. It was all about these Belgian drug smugglers. I had to ask Jessica where Belgium was, and she told me, and of course she had a story about having been there. During the movie though, my mind started to wander. I wondered what Dontae usually did on his weekends. Maybe they sucked, and the only fun thing he did was go to school and get to hear somebody read to him. That made me feel awful, and now he was really sick in the hospital, so it was probably even worse for him. And he couldn't even tell his mom or the nurse or anybody, "Hey, this really sucks."

For a while I imagined being like him. I was in a wheelchair and couldn't walk. I couldn't speak that well either. Damn, living my life was hard enough the way it was, but being like that would be sad. I don't know how I'd make it. I got scared thinking about it. All of a sudden Jessica started clapping excitedly. The movie was over.

Casey dropped me off in front of Jesse's, and Jessica jumped out to say bye. She gave me a long hug, and I hugged her back. I guess because her dad was around all afternoon, she didn't smell like cigarettes. She smelled like some fruity perfume. It was nice, and her hair was soft.

"Your hair smells nice without the smoke," I mentioned.

"Really? I can't tell."

"Just something I noticed."

"See you tomorrow, Javier–Twentieth Century," she said.

"Bye."

They drove off, and I walked up the steps to Jesse's. He came out holding a full dinner plate before I got to the door, so we sat on the steps of the porch.

"Well?" he asked.

"It was cool."

"Get anywhere?"

I knew what he meant, but I wanted to keep him guessing.

"What do you mean?"

"First base? Second base? Home run?"

For some reason I didn't want to lie about Jessica, even if I was just joking with Jesse.

"Nah. It's not like that. She's cool. We just went to the movies," I said.

"Oh." Jesse took a forkful of rice, chewed, and then swallowed. Then he said, "You must like her."

"What?"

"When a guy doesn't want to talk trash about a girl, he likes her."

"She's cool and all, but I don't know if I like her."

"Well, like her or not, by this time tomorrow the whole school is going to know you're going out."

Jesse was right. That's the way it was at school. It didn't matter if you were really a couple or not, just the fact that you did something together meant you were going out. I didn't care though. With the next day being Monday and all, the only thing I was thinking about was what was up with Dontae.

The next day, the news was out. From first period on, I had kids I didn't even know coming up to me and asking if Jessica was my girlfriend. A couple of the girls who were Mexican gave me a hard time about it because Jessica was white and all.

"He don't like his own people!" one of them said during Mrs. McHalenn's class.

I didn't feel like arguing or explaining, especially to some girls who'd never even said hi to me before in the first place. A couple of guys I didn't know gave me high fives too. Then Enrique and some other eighth-graders started talking smack about me and Jessica, but I blew them off. I'd known that it was coming from the moment I agreed to go to the movies.

When Jessica and I partnered up in Mr. O'Neil's to work on our project, some of the girls started whispering and pointing fingers. Jessica didn't care though; she didn't miss a beat. That's when I noticed how strong a person she was. She mentioned something about being pissed with Latrice for telling a couple of people that we went to the movies, but other than that, she was her usual self. But there was one thing different: she didn't smell like smoke. I wondered if it had anything to do with what I'd said about her hair smelling nice.

Even though I tried not to think about it all morning, reality was waiting for me in Mrs. Aronson's class. It was the first time since my first day that I didn't want to walk through the doors of her classroom, 'cause I wasn't ready to hear bad news. I thought about ditching altogether, but then I remembered what happened the last time I tried that. So I nervously made my way to the classroom.

When I got there, I took a deep breath before I opened the door. Instantly my eyes shot to Dontae's work area. His desk was neat, and there was nobody behind it. Mrs. Aronson was at her desk though. She sat behind a stack of paperwork. Her hair was messier than normal, and it looked like she was concentrating real hard to do her work. Cautiously, I walked over to her.

"Hi, Javier," she said with a tired voice, barely looking up from her papers.

When she did glance up, I noticed gray bags under her eyes. She'd never had them before. And when she spoke to me, her voice sounded weak.

"Hi."

"I have to finish these evaluations. I have two strategy sessions this afternoon for Lanzo and Tayshaun. I'll fill you in on Dontae right before you leave. Until then, could you please help Nena?"

"Sure," I said.

141

Making my way over to Nena's desk, I started to get sadder, not just for Dontae, but for Mrs. Aronson too. She'd probably been stressed out all weekend. And the news about Dontae most likely wasn't very good or she would have told me right away. Over the time I'd spent working in her classroom, I got the sense that Mrs. Aronson thought of Dontae as one of her kids. He was technically an eighth-grader, so she'd had him in her class almost two years. I figured she was probably pretty attached to him.

Nena didn't seem herself either. Actually, the whole class was quieter than usual. I signed "hi" to Nena, and she did the same. When I asked her how she was doing, she signed "fine," but her eyes didn't match her words.

By the end of class, Mrs. Aronson was still working on that pile of papers. Again I was cautious as I approached her desk. I tried to think positive, but I kept thinking the worst at the same time. Mrs. Aronson kept her eyes down as she spoke to me.

"Do you know what a trach is, Javier?" she said, and then she took off her glasses to look up at me.

"No."

"In an emergency when somebody can't breathe, they make a cut right here," she said as she pointed to her throat, "and they place a tube there so air can get in."

"Oh," I replied.

"Well, Dontae had to have one when he got to the hospital. He had a bad infection, and it became pneumonia over the weekend. So he's still sick, but he's hanging in there."

"Oh."

"He's on antibiotic medicines to fight the infection, and they're working hard on him. But he probably won't be back to class for a long time."

"Oh," I said, trying not to cry.

"You did an excellent job of helping out during the emergency. I wanted to say thank you."

"No problem."

Mrs. Aronson reached into a drawer in her desk and pulled out a minicassette tape and a recorder.

"I was wondering if you could do me a favor?" she asked.

"Sure."

She handed me the tape and recorder.

"I know you're almost done with the book that you're reading with Dontae. I was wondering if you could record your reading so he has something to listen to. I'm going to get him some other audiobooks, but I think he'd like to hear the end of your story."

"Sure."

"Thanks, Javier. See you tomorrow."

"All right."

Suddenly Mrs. Aronson said, "Oh! And one last thing. I picked you for next semester. It's your choice though. You don't have to be my aide if you don't want to, but I went ahead and put in for you again."

"'Again'? You picked me the first time?" I asked.

"Yes."

"Why?"

Mrs. Aronson took a few seconds to find the right word. Then she said simply, "Empathy."

"Empathy? What's that?"

"It means you have the ability to put yourself in somebody else's shoes, shoes that aren't your own."

"How do you know I got that?"

"The first time you saw my students, you were able to see for one of them. Remember that book Lanzo wanted in the library? You knew what he wanted by what his eyes said to you. That nonverbal communication meant that you were tuned in to what he needed. That's crucial for working with my students."

Nodding, I remembered that first time I'd seen Mrs. Aronson's class the very first week of school. I had forgotten that she'd noticed me helping Lanzo. So I'd ended up in the special ed class for a reason.

"And also because you empathize all the time," Mrs. Aronson continued. "You love to do it. You'd even steal to do it."

I frowned. But suddenly what she was saying made sense. That day she'd caught me red-handed stealing the *Islands* book. It was reading that she was talking about. She meant that reading was another way of experiencing empathy because you start to feel what the people in the stories are going through. For a few seconds my head was spinning. If my life had been a chess game, Mrs. Aronson would have had me checkmated the first time she met me. I didn't know what to do. I guess she must have sensed that 'cause she spoke up.

"See you tomorrow, Javier."

"Bye. Oh, and yeah. I want to come back," I said. Then I turned around and left.

That night, before my mom got home from work, I recorded the rest of the *Islands* book for Dontae. It made me sad to do it like that, but at least he'd be able to hear the rest of the story.

I felt like something was missing that whole week at school, but there was nothing I could do about it. Every day I'd ask Mrs. Aronson how Dontae was, and she'd say the same thing: "He's hanging in there." The other thing on my mind was that our social studies project was due Friday. Jessica had been working really hard to make it professional looking. I'd written all the narration for it, and she did just about everything else. She'd found pictures, videos, and actual songs from the artists. Then we spoke my narration into a microphone, and she edited all of it together. When it was done, the video turned out to be seven minutes long.

On Friday during social studies Jessica was more excited than I'd ever seen her. She kept grabbing my hand and squeezing it. When Mr. O'Neil finally played our project, she got really nervous and seemed to watch everybody's reaction at once. The video looked really cool. Everybody liked it. And when it was all over, Mr. O'Neil shook his head in disbelief and said, "Wow!"

That was all Jessica needed to hear. She gave me a high five. I could see right then and there how much the assignment meant to her, and what she had meant before about her being obsessed with details and a viewable result. She really was special ed in a way, in that the only things that she could really focus on were ones she could make and see. I felt lucky to be her partner because we aced that part of our grade. I got a solid A in social studies for the semester, all because our project rocked. It was the best grade I'd ever gotten in any class, ever.

But the fun of getting a good grade only lasted that period. It was a week after the emergency with Dontae, and Mrs. Aronson still wasn't herself. Every day after school she headed over to the hospital to check on him. I overheard her mention to the aide that sometimes she stayed with him until eight at night. I couldn't think of anything to say to make her feel better, so that week I just tried to be more helpful than I usually was.

It was the last day before Christmas break, and I was feeling miserable. I guess what was really bothering me was that Thanksgiving break was just a week long, but Christmas would be almost three weeks of not getting to work with Dontae and the others. I was going to miss them over the holidays. Mrs. Aronson loaded me up that Friday with about twenty books to read. Once again, she picked out half and I picked out the other half. At least I had some good stories to bring home.

# CHAPTER 13

It turned out that Christmas break wasn't as bad as I thought it was going to be. I had plenty of books to read, Springer in the afternoons, and Jesse and Jessica to hang out with. Most days Jesse would call in the morning to get me to go on a soda-run with him. Then Jessica would call at night to tell me about her day. Her days were pretty much like mine except that she didn't read books all that much. She'd surf the net for hours, listening to music or fact-finding on Wikipedia. A few times we even went to eat.

Sometimes Latrice would go with us, so she and Jessica would sit together in the back of the truck, and I would sit up front with Casey. When the two of them were together, it was like they were in their own little world, and Casey and I were a couple of third wheels just along for the ride. Little by little I noticed a change in the way Casey saw me. That look in his eyes changed to "Now you know what I gotta go through with Jessica." He'd even talk to me about regular things. One time I mentioned my pop's Plymouth, and he got all excited and didn't want to talk about anything else for like thirty minutes. Then the next time we all went out together, he had these car books on the Plymouth he gave me to give to my pop. I guess he really dug cars 'cause that was the official turning point with him. From then on, we were cool.

My mom had Christmas Day off, so we opened presents and watched TV. I got a couple of sweatshirts, a heavier jacket for cold weather, and a layaway slip for a laptop from my mom's work. For her I got one of those musical Christmas cards and a box of chocolates that was gift wrapped. I'd seen them at the convenience store with Jesse, so we each bought a box for our moms with the leftover money from Eduardo. My mom got so happy that she started to cry. And no, there was no way I was going to tell her where the money came from when I saw how happy she was that morning.

Some days while on break, Jesse and I sat on the steps to the apartment. I would read, and he would sneak around back to get high in the alley. It made the time go by easier. One day after Christmas, he showed up carrying a large shopping bag. Before sitting down, he handed the bag to me and made a joke about him being Santa Claus.

"What is it?" I asked him.

"Open the bag."

I looked inside and pulled out a shoe box. My jaw dropped as I saw a brand-new pair of old-school black suede Pumas. They were plush with gold lettering. They had to have been worth a hundred bucks at least.

"No way!" I said, holding the shoes in disbelief.

"Nice, aren't they?" he replied.

"Where'd you get 'em? How'd you get 'em?"

He pointed down to my worn-out Chuck T's. They had faded to dull gray, and there were little threadbare patches on the sides.

"You needed a new pair. Those Chuck T's were getting your ass kicked, so I thought you should try something else," he said with a chuckle.

"But how'd you get these?" I repeated, knowing he couldn't afford them.

"Remember Eduardo bought all those shoes before he got locked up? Well, I thought about all those sneakers just sitting in his room, and here you needed a new pair. I told Eduardo's mom that I lent him a game and wanted it back. She let me go up to his room, so I grabbed some stupid game I found lying around and jacked the Pumas while I was in there. She was in the kitchen when I left the house. She didn't even see what I was carrying out."

"Oh, man! These are too fresh."

Jesse nodded. "I only saw him wear them a couple of times. Go ahead. Try them on. He wouldn't care. He'd want you to wear them."

Quickly I yanked off my old Chuck T's and threw them to the ground. I slid my feet into the new sneakers and laced them up, and man, did they felt nice.

"Awesome," Jesse said as he looked at the shoes. "I should have kept them for myself."

They looked even fresher on my feet than they did in the box.

"Thanks, man. I owe you."

"Shit! You don't owe me. You sobered me up on Halloween, remember?"

"Yeah."

Then Jesse said something that I'll never forget.

"What's wrong with you, Javier? You're always wearing somebody else's shoes!" he said, and then started laughing.

I shook my head and started laughing too. Just then I noticed Jesse twisting a twig between his fingers. I was shocked that he wasn't getting buzzed.

"What? No herb?"

"I'm cutting back."

"How come?"

"I don't know. Ever since the drive-by I've been thinking about quitting. I guess I want to know what's going on too. Maybe you're rubbing off or something."

When Jesse said that, I grinned like crazy because I never thought I had anything that he could want.

Before I knew it, I was back at school. It was like my first day of middle school all over again, except that I knew where to go. Over the holidays I hadn't heard any updates on Dontae. I kind of figured if something major had happened, Mrs. Aronson would have called me, so I'd tried not to think about it. But I still did anyway. I wondered if he might be back in class. When I got to Mrs. Aronson's door that day and looked to his work area though, he wasn't there.

"No," Mrs. Aronson spoke up. "He's not back yet, but welcome back to you."

I gave her a nod.

She told me the latest news on Dontae. He was doing better, but he was still weak from all he'd gone through. Maybe if everything went all right with him, he'd make it back in a couple of months. I was sad to hear that he'd be out that long, but I was still glad that he was doing better.

After telling me the news, Mrs. Aronson handed me the two big tangible symbol notebooks so I could work with Nena. I took them and made my way over to her desk. She was busy trying to write her name five times and didn't see me until I sat down in front of her.

Then she looked up, squinted through her thick glasses, and smiled. Excitedly she signed "hi," and I signed "hi" back.